SAMURAI
OF
GOLD
HILL

SAMURAI
OF
GOLD
HILL

by Yoshiko Uchida

Illustrated by Ati Forberg

Charles Scribner's Sons · New York

For Marty and Ferol
and for Fern Sayre

Contents

THE SECRET PLAN

It was the fourth month of the Year of the Serpent, 1869, and a fine spring rain fell softly over the town of Wakamatsu deep in the Bandai-Azuma mountains of Japan.

In a farmhouse at the edge of town, Koichi peered out at the rainy evening wondering why his father was so late. Taking a paper umbrella and a lantern, he slipped into his straw sandals and went to look down the dark road. Suppose something had happened to Father. Koichi felt once more the cold weight of fear that had overwhelmed him so often since the terrible battle for the castle last fall.

He rubbed his nose with the back of his hand and pulled his homespun kimono close around him. Then, almost without thinking, he looked toward the great black shadow that was the castle of Lord Matsudaira who had ruled over their town. In the darkness he could not see the bullet marks on the white plaster walls or the charred timbers of the massive gates, but he knew that the castle that had soared over their town like a beautiful gold-crested eagle was no longer the proud fort that once protected them. Like the rest of the town it had been badly battered by the southern clans, but at least it still stood.

Koichi thought of the cluster of samurai homes just beyond

the granite base and moat of the castle. They were now only charred piles of rubble and Koichi's home was among them. Koichi shuddered as he remembered the futile battle when, for seven terrible days, the castle and the Aizu Clan had lain in siege. They had been bombarded night and day by the artillery of the southern clans, who, after many years of rule by the Shogunate, wanted the Emperor returned to power. They mercilessly attacked those northern clans who believed that it was the Shogun who should continue to rule. Even now, Koichi could smell the death and defeat that had hovered over everything then.

Father had ridden off to that battle, brave and noble, in his armor and helmet, proudly wearing his two samurai swords and carrying a spear bearing the Matsudaira banner. The last thing he had said before he rode off on his black stallion was, "Be very careful, Koichi, and take good care of Grandmother."

Koichi had nodded solemnly, wishing more than anything else that he could ride off to battle with his father as his older brother had done. But if he had, he would not be here now, for his brother and the entire White Tiger Unit of boys not even seventeen had died in battle.

Koichi and his grandmother had escaped to a farmhouse at the edge of town where Father came back to them with a terrible wound in his left arm and a glazed emptiness in his eyes. The southern clans had stripped him of his armor and his weapons and his steed. He was no longer a proud samurai warrior, but only an exhausted, defeated soldier, whose lord and commander had been captured and sentenced to imprisonment. It was a miracle that Father was still alive.

Koichi prayed each morning for the soul of his mother, who had died when he was born, and now he prayed for the soul of his sixteen-year-old brother, who had died in battle. He did not want to have to pray for the soul of his father as well.

Father had gone off early in the morning, saying only that he had some urgent business to attend to and that he was going with Lord Matsudaira's advisor, Herr Schnell. Koichi wasn't sure he could trust the big green-eyed Prussian. He had sold arms to Lord Matsudaira and had even married the daughter of one of the court samurai, but still, even Father seemed to have some doubts about him.

Koichi wondered if the two of them had gone somewhere to plot the recapture of the castle and the rescue of Lord Matsudaira. If ever there was to be another battle for the castle, Koichi thought, he would be there. He was only twelve, but he was strong and as brave as any samurai son. He had been trained at the castle school to fight with sword and spear. He knew how to use a bow and arrow with grace and skill, and could handle a horse as well as his older brother. He had been trained, furthermore, to think and act as a samurai. He would be brave and dignified at all times and, above all, loyal to his lord. If he captured an enemy warrior, he would permit the man to die with honor, by his own sword. If only he could have a chance to show his skill, Koichi thought forlornly.

He was about to turn back to the farmhouse now, when he saw the faint flicker of a lantern coming toward him. He hurried down the road, slippery and soggy from the rain, and waited for the bobbing lantern to approach. Soon he heard the sound of sandals stepping into the sucking mud and the heavy breathing of one who had walked a long way.

"Father?" Koichi called into the darkness.

"Yes. I have returned."

Koichi sighed with relief. "I'm glad you're back," he said. And they hurried toward the farmhouse together.

Grandmother was sitting close to the oil lamp, which lent only a feeble light to the mending she did. Both she and the farmer's wife worked into the night until it was time to get the quilts from the cupboard and spread them on the floor to sleep. The farmer's wife was weaving hemp and the farmer too was hard at work, twisting strands of rope from rice straw. They all stopped their work when they heard Father's voice at the entrance, and Grandmother hurried to the entrance to help him with his rain-soaked straw cape.

"*Mah, mah,*" she said sympathetically, "you must be weary." And she urged him to come inside quickly.

The farmer's wife stirred the charcoal in the open hearth and heated the black pot that hung over it. Grandmother poured hot water into the pot of fragrant green tea, and the farmer brought Father's tobacco box so he might refresh himself with a smoke.

They were all eager to hear what had happened, for they knew Father had been on an important mission, but first, they attended to his comfort. When Father had eaten two steaming bowls of buckwheat noodles and had some pickled radish with his tea, he began to speak, and they all leaned close to listen.

"Herr Schnell has a plan," he began. "It is a most ambitious plan—one that makes my head swim and my heart anxious."

"Then it is not good?" Koichi asked.

Father thought a moment. "It may hold great good if it is successful," he said carefully, "but for now, we do only what seems best for Lord Matsudaira."

"You have seen him then?" the farmer wondered.

"No, we could not," Father explained, "but Herr Schnell has communicated with him and knows his wishes." Father stopped now, as though not quite sure how much more to tell.

The farmer and his wife lowered their eyes and did not look at Father. He was a samurai, high in Lord Matsudaira's court, while they were only peasants. They did not wish to be unseemly in their curiosity. And Grandmother, although she was of the noble class, did not speak either, for she was only a

4

woman. As for Koichi, he knew that a child listened and did not question.

They waited for Father to speak when he was ready, and he seemed to be sorting the words in his head before he spoke. Finally, looking at the farmer and his wife he said, "You have been most kind to us since the day of the terrible battle. You took in my mother and son and then myself. You allowed us to share the little you possessed. I shall always be grateful."

Koichi wiggled his toes impatiently. He wished Father would hurry and say what he had to say.

"But now," Father went on, "the time has come for my son and me to leave."

"Leave?" The word burst from Koichi like an explosion in the night.

Grandmother caught her breath and put a hand to her mouth. She had noticed that Father had not included her.

"Koichi and I must go on a long journey," Father continued, and then he spoke gently to Grandmother. "Good Mother, I must ask you to wait here for the time being. The plan entails long days of weariness which I cannot ask you to undertake."

Grandmother nodded. "I understand, my son," she said. "When will you and Koichi leave?"

"Very soon now," Father answered. "There is little time and much to do."

Long after the embers in the hearth had been covered with ash and the lamps blown out, Koichi, like each of the others, lay awake on his quilt. Father had not said where they were going, but he had asked Grandmother to prepare enough food and clothing for a long journey. Could they be going as far as Tokyo, the capital city, where now the Emperor reigned instead of the Shogun? Could it be that they were going to join in another battle?

Koichi had never been outside of Wakamatsu before. His

6

heart began to pound at the mere thought of such a trip and he simply had to know now. He sat up on his quilts and glanced toward his father, but the only sound coming from his quilts were those of sleep, and Koichi slid back into his own, filled with impatient curiosity.

The next day Father was gone again, and this time when he returned, he had a horse. He also carried a small drawstring leather bag which he immediately put away with great care.

"Is that sad-looking horse taking us on our journey?" Koichi asked. He had never seen a more pitiful creature, but horses were hard to find now, for the southern warriors had taken away most of those that hadn't been killed in battle.

"That is our hope," Father said with a wan smile. "I hope he will be up to it."

"How far will he have to go?" Koichi asked quickly, seeing that it was a good time to find out where they were going.

"To Tokyo," Father answered.

"To ask the Emperor to give the castle back to Lord Matsudaira?"

Koichi asked the question, knowing even as he did, that such a thing was impossible. One would have to be a very great lord and one who had supported the southern clans to even get near the Emperor's court.

Father shook his head quickly. "You can be sure our plan has nothing to do with His Imperial Majesty, Koichi," he said. And then he added, "We will go on from Tokyo to Yokohama."

"To the port city?" Koichi asked. "Why?"

But Father was not ready to tell him anything more, and Koichi was left with an even bigger puzzle than the night before. All he could do now was get ready to leave and that was easily done, for Koichi possessed scarcely more than the clothes on his back.

7

Grandmother, however, had planned carefully. For many days before the enemy attacked, she had been preparing the things she would take if it became necessary to flee from their house. She had wrapped everything in large heavy silk *furoshiki* bundles. She took one of them out now and removed Father's and Koichi's black silk kimonos bearing their family crest. She also took out a long box that contained Grandfather's samurai swords.

"You are now the only remaining son of the Matsuzaka family, Koichi," she said gravely. "These swords are yours. But for the journey take only one and keep it in remembrance of your grandfather and me."

Koichi knew then that Grandmother must know more than he did, for she spoke as though she might not see him again.

"But we will be back one day, won't we, Grandmother?" Koichi asked.

Grandmother held a thin hand over her mouth, covering the teeth she had carefully blackened, as was the custom, on the day she was married. "Perhaps, my child, perhaps," she said softly, but she said nothing more.

Now she placed the beautiful sheathed sword on top of Koichi's formal kimono, and wrapped them together in a silk *furoshiki*. Then, bowing as she would have done to Father, she slid the packet across the matted floor to Koichi.

"Thank you, Grandmother," Koichi said.

Although he did not know it then, it was to be his Grandmother's last gift to him.

THE JOURNEY BEGINS

The secret plan seemed more strange each day, for now Rintaro, the head carpenter for the castle, seemed to be involved as well. Morning and night he came to hold hurried, whispered conversations with Father and then he disappeared quickly without even stopping to talk to Koichi. This was strange, for as long as Koichi could remember, Rintaro always found time to talk with him.

Sometimes it was when Rintaro hurried to the castle with his crew of roofers, plasterers, sawyers and stonemasons, and sometimes it was when Rintaro came to do some work on their house. He would arrive with a towel twisted around his head, carrying an armful of planes, saws and mallets, and would leave great curls of wood scattered everywhere in his wake.

Always when he saw Koichi he would ask, "Well, are you studying the Chinese classics like a good young samurai?" or "Are you now a master of Confucian thought? Have you learned well the strategy of spear fighting?"

And whatever Koichi had to say, Rintaro would listen intently, his round suntanned face eager and smiling. Koichi had a feeling that although Rintaro was not a samurai, he knew something about Chinese classics and Confucius himself.

But what could Rintaro have to do with their plan for going to Yokohama, Koichi wondered? Perhaps he was going to build some chests of *kiri* wood so Lord Matsudaira's treasures could be taken to some new hiding place.

The farmer knew Rintaro. Maybe he would know. Koichi ran out of the house and toward the fields, calling to the farmer as he ran.

The farmer was busy turning up the weeds and stubble in his fields, adding ash and compost to prepare the soil. Soon it would be the fifth month and then the fields would be flooded and the young rice seedlings transferred from the nursery beds. By the time the rice is planted, Koichi thought, Father and I will be gone.

The farmer tipped back his flat straw hat and wiped his forehead. He was glad to have a chance to rest for a moment, and he came toward Koichi, his sun-darkened face wrinkling into a broad smile. He squatted down beside Koichi at the edge of the field and looked up at the dark mountains that surrounded them.

"Look," he said, pointing, "the young green is already beginning to show on the maple trees. Spring is almost here."

Koichi nodded, but it wasn't the young maple leaves or spring that mattered to him now. "Do you know why Rintaro has come to see Father?" he asked eagerly. "Has he something to do with the secret plan?"

The farmer thought silently, moving his mouth as though he had to chew his words carefully before he let them out. "I did hear Rintaro say he had been to the shrine to determine a lucky day for starting a journey. Maybe . . . it could be that Rintaro is going with you."

"But why?" Koichi asked. "Do you think maybe we are going to build a new castle for the lord in Yokohama? Could that be it?"

The farmer shook his head. "It is all strange to me too, young master," he said, "but it is not for me to guess what the reason might be. My work now is to plow my fields." And stretching the kinks from his legs, the farmer hurried back to the field, leaving Koichi as puzzled as ever.

That night the farmer's wife prepared a special supper. There was not as much wheat added to the rice as usual to make it go farther, and besides the pot of steaming bean-paste soup, there was salt-dried cod, a snowy mound of grated long radish and a dish of pungent yellow pickled radish as well.

"Fish and soup too?" Koichi asked happily. "Is it a festival day?"

Since the battle there was so little food for anyone, Koichi had almost forgotten what it was like to have more than rice and bean-paste soup for supper.

The farmer's wife smiled at Koichi's pleasure. "Eat well tonight, young master," she said.

And when they sat down to eat, Grandmother passed her portion of fish to Koichi. "I am not very hungry tonight," she said, "and besides you must be strong for your journey."

When Koichi turned to look at her, he was startled to see tears at the edge of her eyes.

"Are we leaving soon then?" he asked Father.

"Tomorrow, before sunrise," he said calmly.

Tomorrow! Then the time had come. There was a strange nervous silence in the farmhouse that night, for everyone was filled with anxious thoughts about what was to come. But Koichi was filled, too, with the strange new excitement of hope for a better life. It seemed he had scarcely gone to sleep, with all sorts of unanswered questions still clamoring inside his head, when he felt Father's hand on his shoulder.

"Koichi," his father said softly, "it is time to go."

It seemed like the middle of the night and it was hard to

throw off the dark blanket of sleep. But Koichi could already smell the bean-paste soup bubbling at the hearth, and he leaped quickly from his quilts. Today, of all days, he must not be late.

No one spoke much as they gathered around the hearth, and instead of eating with them, Grandmother and the farmer's wife sat silently, keeping the bowls filled with soup and bran.

Grandmother had prepared several bundles and a reed basket for them to take, and the farmer's wife had made rice balls with pickled plums and wrapped them in bamboo leaves for them to eat on the way.

Koichi saw that Father did not put on his two swords or dress as a samurai usually did. Instead, he wore a homespun kimono and a farmer's round straw hat. Before the war, it was easy to tell a person's station in life by the clothing he wore, but now samurai, farmer, craftsman and merchant wore whatever he could find, for almost everyone had lost his belongings in the fires that scourged the town after the battle. Now everyone in Wakamatsu looked poor and hungry and cold, and it did not seem particularly strange to see Father looking more like a farmer than a samurai. Koichi himself, in his kimono of hemp and his straw sandals, surely looked more like a farmer's child than a samurai's son.

They gathered around the hearth to say good-bye, but only after Koichi and his father had knelt before the family altar to bid good-bye to their departed family and their ancestors. Then, seated properly on the *tatami* floor matting, they bowed in farewell to Grandmother, the farmer and his wife.

When they rose to go to the front entrance, Grandmother put her arm around Koichi. "Keep well, little Ko-chan," she said fondly. "And do not ever forget, wherever you go, that you are the son of a samurai. Be brave and be loyal, and cherish the spirit of the samurai all your life."

"I will, Grandmother," Koichi said.

"Safe journey, then," she said, and to Father, "Safe journey, my son."

Father secured their bundles on the horse's back and bowed once more to Grandmother. "Keep well, Mother," he said gently.

It was time to go. Koichi was glad and sad, and afraid and eager. He felt mixed up, but could only call out over and over again, "Good-bye . . . *sayonara* . . . good-bye. . . ."

And the voices called back, "Keep well . . . safe journey!"

Koichi looked back again and again as they trudged off down the dark path that led toward the mountain pass, but Father did not allow himself to look back. His lips were pressed together and his eyes looked only straight ahead.

Koichi could see Grandmother and the farmer and his wife standing at the doorway. They bowed and waved, and at last, they were lost in the darkness, but Koichi knew they stood there until he and Father had turned at the bend of the road.

Father walked quickly and silently along the edge of the rice fields toward the heavily wooded mountains that loomed close by. It was quiet and dark, with a slip of a moon still hanging in the sky. Except for the occasional howl of a wolf, there was only the clopping of the horse's hoofs and the soft patter of their sandals on the path still damp from the night mist.

They moved on, up a wooded path, and began the climb into the mountains. It was only when they reached the cluster of boulders by the mountain pass that Father stopped and looked down at the town.

Koichi could make out the fields and the makeshift huts and shacks where many of the people lived after their homes were burned. Here and there, a few fires flickered as farmers began to stir with the new day. Koichi wondered how long it would be before he saw Wakamatsu again.

"We will rest here a while," Father said quietly, "and wait for Rintaro."

So he was coming with them after all. "Will he go with us to Yokohama?"

"Yes," Father answered, "and we will meet the others there."

"The others? There are more?"

But now they heard the sound of quick steps and Father put a finger to his lips.

"I have come," a voice called to them in the darkness.

It was Rintaro, panting heavily under the weight of the bundle on his back. "*Sah,*" he said with a quick grin, as he added his bundle to those on the horse's back. "Let us be on our way. Our new life begins."

Father put a hand on his shoulder. "I am glad you are going with us, Rintaro," he said.

"So am I," Koichi added. Somehow now, the journey did not seem such a lonely one.

A LONG WALK

Father took a long last look at the quiet town they were leaving behind and then turned away and led the horse up the narrow mountain trail. The sky was growing lighter now and the sun was close to the crest of the eastern ridge. The birds had already begun to stir, and hearing them, Father quickened his pace, as though reminded of the passing of the hour.

They moved on, quickly and quietly, for what seemed to Koichi many hours, and the thick mass of damp pine needles cushioned their path for them. As they trudged on, Koichi found himself thinking more and more about the rice balls with their red pickled plum hearts. How good one would taste right now with a steaming cup of tea. He swallowed hard, and then reminded himself that a samurai does not concern himself with thoughts of hunger.

At last they came to a mountain stream and Father stopped so they could take a rest and have a cool drink. Koichi sank down on his haunches and was relieved to see Father reach for the bundle that carried their rice balls.

"*Sah,*" Father said, relaxing for the first time that morning, "I think we might have a little food now."

Koichi was so hungry, he ate four rice balls before he could stop to ask Father what he longed to know.

"Father," he began as he bit into his fifth rice ball, "who are the others? Who else is going with us to Yokohama?"

Now that they were safely on their way, Father did not seem so reluctant to talk. "There will be about thirteen of us," he answered.

"All from Wakamatsu? Who are they? Do I know them?" Koichi squeezed in as many questions as he dared.

"Well, there is Herr Schnell and his wife and daughter and maid. Then there is one other carpenter besides Rintaro, and three farmers and two craftsmen."

"Plus you and me," Koichi counted. "What are we going to do in Yokohama, Father?"

"If all goes well," Father said slowly, "we start on still another journey."

Another journey! Koichi was speechless. And before he had time to ask another question, Father stood up and prepared to leave. Rintaro was on his feet too. Koichi followed him to the horse and tried asking him what he ached to know.

"Do you know where we go after Yokohama?" he whispered. "Do you?"

Rintaro put a finger to his lips. "Your father said if all goes well. Sometimes, if one talks too much, it does not go well. Do you see?" And patting Koichi's head as though to put an end to the conversation, he took up the reins and clucked at the horse to get it on its way.

They walked on and on, through forests so thick with cedar and pine, Koichi could scarcely see the sky. They crossed gingerly over rickety wooden bridges that scarcely bore their weight, and sometimes, where there was no bridge, they waded through shallow pebbly streams. Then, slowly, they moved out onto the main road where the great lords of the castle towns had once moved in gilt and lacquered palanquins,

17

surrounded by processions of sword-bearing samurai, chest bearers, stewards and footmen carrying halberds and bows and arrows, and brilliant banners that fluttered with the lords' crest.

Until a few years ago, Father had moved in just such a colorful procession every other year, when Lord Matsudaira went to Tokyo for his year of attendance at the great Shogun's court. In those days, Tokyo was still called Edo, and the Emperor lived in his Kyoto palace, allowing the Shogun to rule the country from Edo. Now the Shogun had retired, there was no lord to rule over their town, and the whole country was in a terrible state of confusion as the new Emperor tried to change Japan from its old feudal ways.

Father thought of the past and spoke now of all that had happened. "It is indeed fortunate that the country is still in chaos," he said, "for if it were not, we could not embark on such a journey as ours. Why only a few years ago, we would have been stopped and questioned at barriers at the edge of every village."

They passed all sorts of people on the road, but no one paid much attention to them, and they spoke to no one. There were other lordless samurai wandering about the countryside, and there were pilgrims on their way to or from the great shrine at Ise. There were priests returning to their temples from distant pilgrimages, and there were peddlers with their packs and old women selling sweetmeats.

Koichi wanted to stop and buy something from every peddler they passed, but whenever he paused and looked longingly at a peddler's pack, Father would shake his head and murmur, "Not now, Koichi, not now."

Koichi knew that Father was being very cautious. Long before they reached the main road, he had taken the drawstring bag from the horse's back and put it inside his kimono. From then on, he walked with a long stick in one hand and the other held firmly over his chest. Whatever it was in that bag, Koichi knew, it must be very precious.

From the second day, Koichi rode the horse for part of each day, and soon Rintaro said he might have to as well.

"My arms have built many a sturdy house," he said with a grin, "but my legs are not used to such hard work." And more than once, Koichi saw him go off by himself to take a quick drink from his sake bottle for added strength.

Sometimes they slept at noisy roadside inns and sometimes at old post stations, where the great processions once stopped for new horses. On other nights, they simply curled up on a bed of pine needles in the quiet depths of a forest, and Koichi would see the stars blinking through the dark dome of pine branches. He would listen to the small insect sounds of the night and then fall into an exhausted sleep.

For ten days and nights they moved steadily on, not daring to be too slow. There were days when the roads became so thick with dust, they had to cover their noses and mouths with towels. Then there were days of rain when the roads became impossible swamps and Koichi wanted to give up then and there.

Each day, however, Father would encourage them, saying, "Well, we are one day's journey closer. We will soon be in Yokohama."

And Rintaro would look down at his shabby sandals and say, "If we do not get there soon, I will have to walk in my bare feet."

At last, one day as the sun slipped lower in the sky, they found themselves on the outskirts of the great bustling city of Tokyo. As they followed one of the three main roads that fed into the city from the north, Koichi saw more people and wagons and horses and carriages than he had ever seen in his life.

By the time they reached the great middle street of the city and came to the Bridge of Japan from which distances to all parts of the empire were measured, Koichi forgot how tired he was.

"Look! Look there! Father! Rintaro, just look!" There were sights such as Koichi had never seen in the little town of Wakamatsu. They crossed bridges laid over wide rivers and muddy ditches, and in the distance, they saw the great castle towering over the moats and bridges and enormous stone embankments that protected it.

"There it is!" Koichi shouted. "The Shogun's castle."

"Not anymore," Father reminded him. "It is the Emperor's palace now and I will probably never enter it again."

Koichi was too excited to feel Father's sadness. Now they were passing rows and rows of small shops and stalls that lined the streets, and Father took them into a small *oden* shop from which drifted a smell so delicious Koichi forgot every samurai-like thought he had ever been taught about food. The steaming bowl of vegetables and roots and bean curd cooked in broth sent new strength coursing through them and gave them the energy to walk on to Yokohama.

It was dark when they reached the busy port city, but even then, they could feel its bustling activity, for it was visited regularly now by ships from the western world. They walked down the main road, and Father pointed out the official Japanese buildings on one side of the road and, on the other, the two-storied consulate offices of the foreign countries that now traded with Japan.

Koichi stared in amazement. How could a city in Japan look so utterly different from Wakamatsu? It was almost as though he were in some foreign land.

Father told them how the city had been a swampy marsh not so long ago. But now what Koichi saw was a vast confusion of shops and stalls, where carpenters, dyers, umbrella makers, tea packers, sake brewers, tailors, boat repairers and wharf porters were jammed together working side by side. Even more amazing was the recreation area built on another part of the swamp for the foreign residents whose elegant homes stood high on the bluff overlooking the harbor.

Rintaro was as amazed as Koichi. "So this is where all the hairy barbarians live," he mused aloud, and he looked from left to right and up and down, scarcely daring to blink for fear of missing something.

Koichi, too, was so busy looking around, he scarcely noticed when Father stopped.

"Well, here we are at last," Father said. "We have arrived at Herr Schnell's import shop."

Sure enough, they were standing in front of a small shop with a sign in the window which read J. HENRY SCHNELL, IMPORTER.

Father slid open the door and called, "Herr Schnell, it is Matsuzaka, Gentai. We have arrived."

And from somewhere in the back of the shop came the thick accented voice of J. Henry Schnell.

"Come in, come in. You have arrived just in time."

AN OCEAN TO CROSS

It was the first time Koichi got such a close look at Herr Schnell. Many times he had seen him hurrying to or from the castle, but never before had he stood just inches away from him. Koichi was surprised to find him so large and so tall. He towered over Father like a great lumbering animal, making Father look frail and small.

Herr Schnell bowed carefully and spoke in his usual excellent Japanese. He smoked a cigar that filled the shop with a terrible smell, and his voice was so loud Koichi was sure he could be heard halfway down the wharf.

He bent to pat Koichi's shoulder. "So, you have come safely with your father, eh?" And he took the cigar from his mouth long enough to give Koichi a quick smile. In the light of the lamp his curly brown hair and moustache glinted red, and his eyes were the strange yellow-green of a cat's.

Koichi looked carefully at Herr Schnell's shoes. Once, long ago, one of their servant women had told Koichi that all the big-nosed foreigners who came to Japan not only had cloven hoofs like animals, but had no heels on their feet. "That is why," she whispered knowingly, "they cannot wear sandals as we do, but must wear shoes that lift up their heels."

Koichi knew that Herr Schnell's feet were not cloven, but he did indeed have heels on his shoes. Someday, when he removed his shoes, Koichi thought, he would have to inspect his feet.

The servant had also told him that all "hairy big-nosed barbarians" ate the meat of cattle and hog and drank the milk of the cow. "That explains their cloven feet," she said, "and that is why they smell of animal fat and butter."

Even now, no one in Wakamatsu ate beef or pork because of their Buddhist beliefs, and although Father explained that meat was very nourishing and was eaten in such cities as Tokyo, Grandmother insisted that she would never do such a barbaric thing as long as she lived.

The idea of slaughtering an animal that lived on one's farm and cutting it up for food did seem rather horrible to Koichi too, and he didn't think he would ever want to drink the white liquid that flowed from a cow.

But now, Koichi saw that Father and Herr Schnell were deep in conversation. He saw Father take the heavy drawstring bag from his kimono and give it to Herr Schnell, who quickly put it into a big safe at the back of his shop.

"Have the others arrived?" Father asked.

"All but two of the farmers," Herr Schnell answered, "and I expect them tomorrow. They are bringing the silkworm eggs."

"And the trees and plantings?"

"They are already safely stowed in the ship's hold."

Koichi dared not interrupt them, but he listened hard with his whole body. Hadn't Herr Schnell mentioned a ship? What were they going to do with trees and plants and silkworm eggs? What did it all mean?

Koichi was about to burst with curiosity. The moment they were outside on their way to an inn, he turned to Father.

"What ship, Father?" he asked. "What are the trees and

23

plants for? What is going to happen? Where are we going? Father!"

The words came rushing out like water freed from a dam.

Rintaro too was full of questions. "Is it all settled now? Is our ship to sail soon?"

Father answered Rintaro first. "I believe we sail tomorrow night," he said, and then he turned to Koichi with a smile.

"Now that we have come safely to Yokohama, I can tell you of our great dream. Listen well, Koichi. Tomorrow we board the ship *China* of the Pacific Mail Steamship Lines. Then we sail across the ocean to America and go to Gold Hill in the state of California. Herr Schnell has written many letters to America and believes that Gold Hill would be a fine place to establish a tea and silk farm. Think of it, Koichi," Father said, his eyes dancing now with excitement, "we shall be the very first colonists from Japan to go to America to farm."

Koichi's head was reeling. They were going to America. They were actually leaving the shores of their own country, when not too many years before, it would have been against the law of the land.

"Will we not be beheaded for leaving the country?" Rintaro worried, still remembering how it was when no foreign ships were even permitted to come to Japanese ports.

Father shook his head. "It is all different now, Rintaro. Besides, with our country in such confusion, no one will even know we have left."

Rintaro murmured wonderingly. "Such a wild dream," he said almost to himself.

"What of Lord Matsudaira?" Koichi asked now. "What about our castle? Won't we fight once more to get the castle back for our clan?"

"Lord Matsudaira is imprisoned, but at least he lives," Father said quietly. "From now on, there will be no more battles, for Japan must live in peace." Then lowering his voice, he added, "We go to America to establish a sanctuary for the lord. Perhaps one day he will be free to join us there. Don't you see, Koichi, we are still his loyal subjects, but now we serve him with our labor instead of our swords."

Father touched his chest where he had kept the drawstring bag during the long trip. "The lord gave us two thousand pieces of gold which were not taken by the southern clans," he explained. "With that we can buy land and tools and food and begin a Wakamatsu Colony in America. Herr Schnell has arranged it all."

So that was it. The drawstring bag was filled with gold. The plants and trees in the ship's hold were for their new farm.

"Is it not a magnificent plan?" Father asked. Koichi hadn't seen such brightness in his eyes since before the big battle.

But still Koichi felt confused. He was filled with excitement at the thought of the great new adventure that lay ahead, but he also felt a strange disappointment. It simply didn't seem right for Father to be leaving Japan to become a farmer. He was a superb horseman. He could handle any weapon with skill and grace. He was a scholar in Chinese classics and could speak Dutch and a little English and French as well. He would be a perfect teacher, but how could he pick tea leaves or till the soil or care for silkworms? A samurai did not do such things. They were tasks for a farmer or a woman, at best.

All his life Koichi had dreamed of becoming one day a noble samurai like his father. It was for this that he went to the castle school to study the classics, to learn calligraphy and to excel in the skills of war and self-defense. He dreamed of one day defending the lord and his castle, just as Father had done. Now, Koichi wondered, what was to become of him? He thought of the samurai sword Grandmother had given to him. Perhaps he would never have a chance to use it, and it would rust in its gilt and lacquer sheath while he picked mulberry leaves for silkworms.

Father seemed to know what troubled Koichi. "A good samurai always serves his lord," he reminded him, "and if that service brings some disappointments that, too, is accepted in good grace."

Koichi nodded. He knew all that, but still he could not be entirely happy over the idea of becoming a farmer.

When they went to the wharf the next day to board the ship, however, Koichi began to feel an overwhelming surge of excitement. He saw the ship's towering masts and the giant side-wheels and thought it seemed like a small floating castle. And when they met the others who had also come from Wakamatsu, he did not feel so much the terrible tug of loneliness at the thought of leaving Japan.

Herr Schnell's beautiful Japanese wife was already on the ship with her daughter, Toyoko, and her maid, Okei.

"Perhaps you will become friends—you and my little Toyoko?" Mrs. Schnell said, speaking so softly Koichi barely heard her.

Koichi nodded, but he did not say yes. After all, Toyoko was only eight, and worse, she was a girl. Koichi wanted no part of a girl's world, and besides, he had Rintaro. During the long journey to Yokohama he was strong and reliable and a cheerful companion. He was not much younger than Father, but Father seemed almost to think of him as another son. And Koichi began to think of him as a big brother to replace the one he had lost in battle.

Rintaro shared their small crowded cabin with one of the craftsmen. He scratched his head as he examined the narrow shelf-like bunks that jutted from the walls.

"Look at these little shelves we must sleep on," he said, laughing. "We must lie still like sacks of rice or we will end up on the floor with broken heads."

"I'm going to put my blankets on the floor," Koichi announced. But Father told him that he must get used to sleeping as the foreigners did. So Koichi crept gingerly onto his shelf, clutched the sides so he wouldn't fall out and fell into a restless sleep, wishing that he had his nice smooth wooden pillow instead of the lumpy one for foreign heads.

When he awoke, he heard the slow creaking sounds of the ship all around him. During the night they had slipped out of the harbor and now Koichi could hear the churning and splashing of the great side-wheels and feel the roll of the ship as it rode the swells of the Pacific. They were on their way.

"*Yah*, we are sailing the ocean now," Koichi shouted, and he quickly followed Father and Rintaro outside into the dizzying, rocking world of sea and spray. He ran to the railing and there it was, the enormous Pacific Ocean, stretching out for endless miles. Nowhere, not even in the far distant horizon, was there even a glimmer of a sliver of land.

They wobbled about the sloping deck and Koichi craned his neck to watch the wind fill the great white sails, billowing like graceful swans in the enormous blue lake of the sky. He saw the smokestack belching great streams of black smoke as the burning coal powered the wheels that pushed them closer to the new land.

The three of them explored the ship from prow to stern like three reeling pioneers in a new and strange land. Then Father turned to Koichi and said a most unexpected thing.

"Now, Koichi," he said very calmly, "let us go see about our treasures."

STRANGE TREASURES

Treasures! Koichi could scarcely wait to see them. There were probably great scented chests of *kiri* wood bearing Lord Matsudaira's crest and secured with thick twisted cords of red silk. Inside, there would be stacks of gold coins, mounds of jade and creamy pearls, precious porcelain bowls, swords glistening sharp and cold, lacquered armor and gold-trimmed spears. Koichi wondered why Father stopped to ask the farmers to go down with them to the hold. Perhaps the chests were heavy and needed many hands to be lifted for inspection.

With one of the ship's sailors leading the way, they moved carefully along the ship's slanting creaking corridors, down narrow stairways and wobbly stepladders, down, down into the dark dampness of the ship's hold. There, they moved in and out among towering stacks of crates, boxes of tea and bales of rice, and came at last to a corner that looked like a battered shabby forest of wind-tipped trees.

"Ah," Father said, "here they are, safe and sound."

"Those mulberry trees?" Koichi asked, disappointed. "Those are our treasures?"

"Indeed they are," Father answered, looking pleased to find them intact. "We have several thousand to start our new farm, and here are the tea plants and the bamboo, lacquer and wax trees. We have brought thousands of seeds of the tea and sesame plant as well."

Seeing the disappointment that flooded Koichi's face, he explained further. "Don't you see, Koichi, they will help us make a living in California. We will harvest the tea and the oil and the wax, and the craftsmen will make bowls and baskets and boxes and ornaments from the bamboo and lacquer."

"And do not forget our precious cargo of silkworm eggs," one of the farmers reminded him.

"For making the most beautiful silk ever made outside of Japan," Father added.

"We had better pray to the gods that they don't hatch before we get to Gold Hill," Rintaro said with a worried frown.

"We had indeed," the farmers agreed. "This is the fifth month of the year and almost time for the eggs to hatch."

With expert hand and eye, the farmers checked their precious cargo and carefully dampened whatever needed water. They also cast an anxious eye on the silkworm eggs, glad for the cool darkness of the hold that would keep them safe until the ship reached America.

"There really are no treasure boxes at all?" Koichi asked, just to make sure.

"That is right, my son. These plants and trees are our treasures now. Without them, we would have no farm and no way to earn a living."

So they really were going to become farmers, Koichi thought glumly. They did not even own one treasure box of swords or spears or armor.

As if that were not bad enough, Koichi learned that he was to study English each day with Toyoko Schnell.

"Herr Schnell has agreed to instruct you each day," Father explained, "so you will be able to speak some English before we reach America."

If Rintaro, who had already learned a little English from Father, hadn't offered to study with him now, Koichi probably would have gone to hide in the ship's hold. He would far prefer the silent company of the damp trees and silkworm eggs to the chattering of Toyoko Schnell with her strange gray eyes and brown-tinged hair. She looked neither Japanese nor Prussian, but was a strange mixture of the two. The people in Wakamatsu had said she would never find a proper husband because she was half barbarian, and they felt sorry too for her Japanese mother, who had become the wife of a foreigner.

"I don't care what she looks like," Koichi confided to Rintaro, "if only she was a boy."

"But she isn't," Rintaro said matter-of-factly, "so you might as well get used to her. She's going to be with us for a long time."

Koichi sighed. What a bother she was going to be. But because she sat beside him and was so much better in English than he, Koichi tried twice as hard and learned English faster than he would have at the castle school.

By the time the ship stopped at the Hawaiian islands for fresh water and coal, both Koichi and Rintaro knew many words of English. They did not get off the ship, but they leaned from the ship's railing and shouted English words down to the men who worked on the dock below.

"*Oi!* I am called Matsuzaka, Koichi. Table and chairs! Thank you! Good night! I am twelve. Coffee!" Koichi shouted down every English word he had learned. They did not hear him in the noise and confusion of unloading the ship's cargo, but Koichi shouted anyway, pleased that he could speak their tongue. In fact, Koichi tried his English on anyone who would listen.

"Good evening," Koichi said one day to Okei as she and Toyoko stood at the ship's stern looking down at the foamy wake left by the ship. Much to Koichi's surprise, Okei answered back in slow careful English.

"Good evening. I am called Okei." Then holding up a hand to cover her mouth, she giggled in embarrassment.

"You are learning English too?" Koichi asked, surprised. There was probably no servant girl in all of Wakamatsu who could speak more than her own native tongue.

Okei shook her head. "I know only a few words that Toyo-chan taught me," she said shyly, holding on to the young girl's hand. "But I wish to learn more."

Okei shivered slightly in the wind and turned once more toward the sunset. "We come here each evening to watch the sunset," she explained. "And we think about how the sun goes on to shine over Wakamatsu, don't we Toyo-chan?"

Toyoko nodded in agreement, but spoke no words. She was still not sure about Koichi even though they studied English together every morning for three hours.

Koichi, however, was not paying attention to her, for he spoke with Okei. She seemed different from the dull, stolid servant girl who used to help Grandmother. Okei's face was gentle and her eyes smiling and bright. Her hair was pulled straight back and tied simply in the manner of most servant girls, and her kimono was of rough homespun. She could not have been more than seventeen, but already her hands were rough and red from years of hard work on her father's land.

"Why did you come?" Koichi asked her now. "You wanted to leave Wakamatsu?"

"Oh no," Okei said quickly. "The Schnell family needed me, so I have come." Okei in her own way was as loyal to the Schnells as Father was to Lord Matsudaira. They had asked her to come and she had not even considered refusing.

"Mama would have wept if you didn't come," Toyoko said now, looking up at Okei. "And so would I."

Okei smiled. "But I am a little afraid," she began.

"Of the foreigners?"

She nodded. "They might shoot us with their cannons," she said fearfully, remembering how their town had been ravaged by weapons supplied by the foreigners.

Koichi spoke up quickly. "We will protect you," he said grandly. "Father and I, with our swords and spears. Don't be afraid," he said. And he strode off manfully, feeling more like a samurai than he had since they left Japan.

The morning they were to dock in San Francisco, Koichi was up before dawn. He didn't want to miss a thing and was eager to be on deck to catch the first sight of land. He wore his good silk kimono as Father had instructed, and he saw that Father, too, wore the kimono bearing the family crest, a long silk divided skirt and a short coat of black silk. With his two samurai swords at his side, he looked at last as a samurai should. Koichi was glad. He didn't want Father to arrive in the new land looking like a shabby peasant.

Okei helped Toyoko's mother do up her hair in glossy black puffs with sweet-smelling camellia oil, and then helped her put on her finest silk kimono and her wide brocade sash. Then she dressed Toyoko and herself, and the three of them looked as though it was New Year's Day and they were about to go to the shrine.

The farmers and the craftsmen, Rintaro and the other carpenter too, all wore their finest clothes and assembled near Herr Schnell at the ship's railing, straining eagerly for the first sight of America. The ship passed through a low bank of fog and then suddenly there appeared what seemed a wall of mountains, and in that wall the captain seemed miraculously to find a small opening through which he steered the *China* into one of America's busiest ports. It was a magnificent sight.

They passed enormous clipper ships and square riggers and

giant rafts piled high with lumber and wheat from the California valleys and forests. There were freighters laden with cargo from all over the world and there were many smaller riverboats. The *China* moved closer to the piers, which extended into the water like giant fingers reaching out for the ships of the world. And then they docked. They had reached their destination. They were in America.

"We're here! We've landed! We are in California!" Koichi shouted, and in his excitement, he forgot that Toyoko was a girl and found himself shouting into her ear. "Look! Look at all the foreigners down there."

"Oh yes," she squealed back in excitement. "I see them!"

The pier was crowded with people and express wagons and handcarts and coaches. And everywhere, shouting and calling, were voices speaking a strange foreign babble. Koichi listened hard. Was it English they were speaking? Koichi suddenly discovered that he could not utter one word of it now. His tongue, it seemed, had frozen in his mouth.

They left the ship together, keeping close to one another. The men strode ahead first, their heads held high. Herr Schnell led the group and Father walked directly behind, looking dignified and composed. Koichi tried to look the same, but his heart was thumping and his throat felt dry. The women came last, lowering their eyes to avoid the curious stares.

Now it was they who were the foreigners, in their rustling silk kimonos, their swords, and their black hair done up in strange hairdos. Koichi felt as though he was in a land of fair-skinned, brown-haired giants. And all of them turned to stare. Some glared and some grinned. One of the men handling cargo stopped working, scratched his head and muttered in disbelief at the sight of people he thought must be Chinese, but who somehow looked different. He didn't even try to work until they had passed by.

Koichi was relieved when they reached their hotel. It was a two-storied wooden structure built on land that had once been a cove.

"Keep your sandals on," Herr Schnell reminded them as they walked gingerly through the front door. "No one removes shoes in this country."

It was strange, Koichi thought, that everyone brought the dirt and dust of the street into their homes, but Herr Schnell explained that it was because they did not use their floors for sitting and sleeping as they did in Japan. "Here they use chairs and tables and beds," he explained.

It seemed strange, too, that there were American flags flying everywhere and red, white and blue bunting decorating the buildings.

"Have we come on a festival day?" Koichi asked.

Herr Schnell himself wasn't sure until he spoke to the hotel clerk, and then he nodded. "Ah yes, the great transcontinental railway was just completed two weeks ago," he explained. "The rails from the east and the west were joined at Promontory Point, Utah, so now a railway spans the entire United States. The flags were put up for the celebration."

"*Mah,*" Toyoko's mother said in amazement, scarcely knowing what a transcontinental railway was.

"Imagine," Father remarked. "An iron horse that can cross a continent."

"I will ride it someday," Koichi said grandly. And then quickly added, "But only to see the country before we go home to Wakamatsu."

As he stood dreaming such dreams, however, Rintaro was ready to go upstairs with their bundles.

"*Sah, sah,* come, Koichi-san," he urged, "let us go up and inspect our first American rooms."

GOLD HILL AT LAST

The room was big and bare, with two large brass beds and a marble-top washstand bearing a basin and pitcher. Koichi had somehow expected more of his first American room.

"I thought . . ." he began and then he stopped. He really didn't know what he thought it would be like. Perhaps he had expected silken screens painted with silver and gold, or lacquered tables inlaid with mother-of-pearl. He had been dreaming of the elegant rooms of the castle at Wakamatsu and thinking America would be even more rich and golden and beautiful.

Their room smelled of stale tobacco and the horses stabled next door.

"Come, Koichi-san, let us go out and inspect this city of the hills," Rintaro said in his loud cheerful voice. "Your father and Herr Schnell have already gone to see about buying supplies and shipping our trees and plants to Gold Hill."

Rintaro asked the other men if they would like to go along, but none of them did. "We will wait here for Herr Schnell," they said cautiously. "We will wait until later."

But Koichi and Rintaro couldn't wait to see the city. They strode out of the hotel together, Rintaro with a short sword thrust in his sash and Koichi with Grandfather's sword dangling at his side.

"Look straight ahead," Rintaro told Koichi. "Do not meet their stares and they will leave us alone."

They marched with their eyes straight ahead past a carriage shop and a warehouse heaped with tallow and hides. But Koichi could not keep looking ahead for long, for now they came to buildings of stone and granite, some of them three stories high, and there were banks and courthouses and theaters and shops on all sides. Koichi simply had to stop at the windows to gaze at the shawls and jewels and tortoise-shell combs for the ladies and the hats and shirts and collars for men.

The streets were full of people, all rushing about as though they were late for appointments. They all took time, however, to stare at the strange-looking pair. Even people in horse-drawn wagons and carriages leaned out to stare as though they couldn't quite believe their eyes.

Rintaro led Koichi up and down the cobbled streets, pausing now and then in front of a saloon where the sound of laughter and music came cascading out into the streets. He licked his lips, looked longingly at the doorway and then at Koichi and, with a sigh, continued to walk straight ahead.

"You can go in if you want to. I won't tell Father," Koichi said loyally.

But Rintaro shook his head. "No," he said. "Today I do no drinking. Besides," he added with a quick grin, "I have only coins of Japan, and here they would not even buy me an empty wine cup."

They walked up and down the streets of San Francisco until they were too hungry to go further. When they got back to their hotel, they discovered that Herr Schnell had ordered a dinner of boiled potatoes, corned beef and cabbage and coffee for them all.

"Ugh," Koichi groaned, as he drank the steaming black liquid. It was bitter and so hot, the tears came rushing to his eyes. And when he picked up the heavy fork and ate a mouthful of corned beef, he could almost hear his Grandmother scolding, "*Mah, mah,* my grandson, eating the meat of a cow!"

"Papa says the meat will make us grow big and strong," Toyoko said as she watched Koichi poking about at his meat.

But when Koichi looked around the table, he saw that all the others were having trouble swallowing their meat as well. Only Herr Schnell was chewing and swallowing busily as though it were a meal fit for Lord Matsudaira himself.

Early the next morning, they boarded another side-wheeler. This time it was a smaller ship called *The Sitka,* and it was to take them up the river to Sacramento.

"From Sacramento we will rent wagons to Placerville," Herr Schnell explained. "And from Placerville, we shall go on to our final destination, Gold Hill."

Koichi liked the name. It sounded as though the hillsides were laden with veins of gold, and even though Herr Schnell had told them the gold rush was over, perhaps he could find just a little gold that no one had discovered before.

The little *Sitka* crept slowly up the river, passing other riverboats and barges laden with wheat coming out from the valleys.

"How dry the countryside looks," Father said, for as far as they could see, the low curved hills, dotted with dark clumps of live oak, were the color of golden sand or ripened wheat.

"There has been no rain here," the farmers said anxiously. "The earth is as dry as a bleached bone."

"Strange that it should be so in the sixth month," Rintaro mused, for in Japan this was the time for the rainy season. Rain fell from dull leaden skies for weeks and weeks, until the land was like a soaking sponge. It was a dreary time of year, but the farmers were glad for the rain-filled paddies where the rice plants would thrive green and strong.

America was not only bigger and noisier, it seemed brighter and sharper, and Koichi felt as though he had come from a land of soft gray mist to a land of eternal harsh sun.

"What about the silkworm eggs?" he asked. "Since it is so warm, won't they hatch and die before we can feed them?"

"I have been thinking of them too," Father said, "but there is nothing we can do. I don't even know if they are on this same ship with us."

"How much farther?" Koichi asked Herr Schnell.

"Not far now," he answered reassuringly, but it was almost dusk when they reached Sacramento, and it was not until early the next morning that Herr Schnell rented three wagons for the ride to Placerville almost fifty miles away.

The crack of the driver's whip sent the horses dashing down the dusty Green Valley road. It was a long bumpy ride, for the road was worn with ruts made by the hundreds of wagons and coaches that had traveled over it during the rush for silver and gold, and by the thundering horses of the pony express.

The horses kicked up a fine spray of red dust, and only Herr Schnell seemed to have the inclination to talk with the driver of the wagon, who was happy to have someone listen to his memories of how it had been during the busy gold rush years. He told of the days when there had been so many wagons moving down the road that if one pulled off the road in the morning, it couldn't get back in line until late at night. He pointed out each village they passed, the old pony express stops and the first farm that owned a mechanical plow.

They moved on, passing clumps of willow and poplar and buckeye and, once in a while, tall pines quite unlike the gnarled trees that stood near the temple at Wakamatsu. Sometimes a rabbit or squirrel would skitter across the road, or a deer would bound away into the woods at the sound of the horses, and once, Koichi saw a large brown bear lumbering slowly into the thickets.

The wagons rumbled on through the heat of the day and came at last to a busy town where they stopped in front of an old two-storied hotel.

"Well, here we are in Placerville," Herr Schnell called out.

Koichi knew it was a fairly big city, for the driver had told them there were over eight good mountain roads running in all directions from it, and on the main street, he had seen banks and newspaper offices and even a telegraph company.

They climbed wearily from the wagons, covered with dust. Mrs. Schnell coughed and fanned herself with a small folding fan. Her beautiful silk kimono was full of wrinkles and her hair grayed with dust.

"Mama, I ache all over," Toyoko groaned.

Koichi felt exactly the same.

"Wait here," Herr Schnell instructed the dreary group. "I must find new wagons to take us to Gold Hill." And he went off down the dusty street.

The terrible searing heat of the afternoon felt like the breath of an angry dragon.

"A nice long soak in a tub would feel good right now," Rintaro sighed, stretching his aching legs.

"And a bowl of rice and pickles," Koichi added.

"I'd rather have a sweet bean-paste cake," Toyoko said.

But Okei was not thinking of food or hot baths. "See how they all stare at us," she murmured. "I do not like the look in their eyes."

"I do not either," Toyoko's mother said, and she drew her child closer to her.

Everyone who went by stopped to stare at them, and one man even spat in the dust at their feet.

"Why do they hate us?" Koichi asked. "What have we done?"

"It is just that they don't know us, that is why they dislike us," Father explained. "When we have built our fine tea and silk farm it will be different. You'll see." Father tried to sound cheerful, but his face was drawn and creased with lines of weariness.

When Herr Schnell came back at last, he had only one wagon and he looked glum. "No one will rent wagons to us," he said darkly.

"Why?" they all wondered.

"Because we are Japanese."

"Ah. And that is bad?"

"They do not know us, so they do not trust us. It is always bad to be different. I was once different too, in your country." Herr Schnell looked tired and discouraged and Koichi suddenly felt sorry for him.

Koichi looked down on the ground because he didn't know what to say. Presently, he noticed an enormous pair of boots beside him. He looked up at the face that belonged to the boots and saw a tall fair-haired man wearing the working clothes of a farmer. His nose was sprinkled with freckles and his eyes were a friendly blue. He wiped his forehead with a big handkerchief and asked, "Say, ain't you the folks from Japan who're coming up to the Graner place in Gold Hill?"

"We are. We are," Herr Schnell answered eagerly.

"Heard you was coming," the man said. "My name's Thomas Whitlow. I'm ranching close by the Graner place." He held out an enormous hand which Herr Schnell shook vigorously.

"We're in need of two more wagons," Herr Schnell explained.

"I can take some of you," Thomas Whitlow offered. "We could do it in two wagons if you folks don't mind squeezing in some."

The gods had sent this kind man just in time, for now the sun was dropping in the sky and the air was growing dusky.

The road to Gold Hill was as bumpy as the Green Valley road, but now the horses jogged along gently for there weren't many miles to go. They passed small villages and farms and dozens of orchards filled with trees bearing apples and plums and peaches and almonds. And on the hillsides were vineyards climbing as high as the water could go.

As they bumped along, Koichi's head dropped to his chest, and the rumbling wagon lulled him to an exhausted sleep. The shadowy trees moved by like silent ghosts and the sounds of the buzzing cicadas began to fill the air.

Koichi dreamed he was in Japan, riding to a great battle to win back the castle. The battle was almost won and Koichi was waving the Matsudaira banner in the air when the wagon pulled off the road and came to a stop.

"Here we are," Mr. Whitlow's voice sang out in the warm darkness. "This here's the Graner place."

They had finally come to the end of their journey. This was the Graner house and this was Gold Hill. The Wakamatsu Colony of Japan had arrived at last.

THE SILENT CELLAR

The Graner house which stood on their land was a tired-looking wooden building with a wide porch that ran the length of the front. It stood close to the road, open and vulnerable, and Koichi was surprised to see that it did not even have a fence to protect it from thieves and enemies.

Behind the house was a small barn and then there stretched open land sloping toward the hills. The land had once been cultivated but was now overgrown with tall dry weeds. Beyond that were thickets and a cluster of trees that held promise of water and shade. A single willow tree, its branches sweeping low to the ground, stood close to the front porch.

Okei frowned as she went by it. "A willow tree is a bad omen," she said anxiously, and Toyoko's mother nodded in agreement. "A willow brings illness and bad fortune," she whispered to her husband.

But Herr Schnell brushed her fears aside. "Nonsense," he said brusquely. "We are in America now and there are no such foolish notions here."

Koichi wondered who was right, but for now he was too tired to think about it. It seemed a small miracle that they had crossed the enormous ocean, traveled up the wide river, journeyed over long, winding roads and had actually arrived at their destination.

"We're really here in Gold Hill," he said, more to convince himself than anything else.

"Yes," Father answered. "We are home at last."

Early the next morning Kate Whitlow arrived with her husband, carrying a basket of fresh eggs, milk, homemade bread and freshly churned butter.

"Put some good food inside you before you go work in the fields," she said, bending to start a fire in their black wood stove.

She was like sunshine on a rainy day with her golden hair and her bright blue eyes. Okei and Toyoko's mother hovered close, watching her pump up water from the well, fill the big kettle and get a wood fire started in the stove without smoking up the whole house. Kate's cheerful voice filled the kitchen as she tried to teach Okei how to prepare an American breakfast.

"See?" she said, filling the coffeepot. "It's easy."

The women nodded and smiled, understanding her motions even though they could not understand her words.

Thomas Whitlow had brought two horses and plows from his farm to help them get started clearing the fields of fallen tree trunks, bleached bones, stubble, weeds and rocks.

"You got a big job to do," he said sympathetically. "You'd best get moving pretty quick to get ditches dug so you can get water from the creek to flow down to your fields."

Herr Schnell had made sure there would be water for their fields and he agreed that they must get to work immediately.

They all hurried out to the fields wearing wide straw hats to shield them from the sun. The farmers knew what needed to be done and they directed the others who until now had worked only with spears and swords or hammers and chisels. Herr Schnell and his wife had never even set foot in a farmer's field before.

They all went out to the fields now with hoes and picks and shovels, Koichi and Toyoko with them. Only Okei and the farmers felt at ease for their backs bent easily to a task they had known before.

"*Yoisho . . . ah yoisho . . .*" the farmers sang out to the rhythm of their digging, but the others found it difficult to keep up. Even Herr Schnell, who was bigger than any of them, was sagging and dripping with sweat before the sun reached its noon peak.

They worked hard in the hot sun, their backs aching, their hands blistered, their throats parched, and when the wagons

bearing their plants and trees arrived in the heat of the day, they worked even harder.

"Koichi, can you tend to the silkworm eggs?" Herr Schnell asked. "I cannot spare anyone from the fields until the trees and plants are set in and watered."

Koichi had watched the farmer's wife in Wakamatsu take care of her silkworms. He knew what to do, but he wanted to stay in the fields with the rest of the men. Tending silkworms was a woman's job.

Herr Schnell looked anxiously at Koichi. "Can you do it?" he asked again. "The larvae are beginning to hatch."

Koichi nodded. When Herr Schnell asked you to do something, you did not say no. Koichi knew now why some of the men called him "Generalissimo."

"I can do it," he said glumly, and putting down his hoe, he headed for the house.

"Toyoko will help you," Herr Schnell called out. "She is small, but she has watched the farm women. She will know what to do."

Herr Schnell had only added insult to injury by sending Toyoko after him. She came running now saying, "I know what to do. They must be put in the cellar in a cool place, and we must chop up some mulberry leaves so they can eat."

"I know," Koichi answered. "I could do it by myself."

Using old crates and boxes for trays, they rushed the larvae onto their new clean beds.

"I'll go pick some mulberry leaves," Koichi said. "You chop them up."

Toyoko nodded obediently. Just as her mother did whatever her father asked, she knew that it was her place to listen to Koichi. He was older, and besides that he was a boy. That put him at least two notches above her in their small world, and she knew it. Being the youngest and a girl at that, she was perhaps the least important person in the whole colony. Watching Kate Whitlow, she had been surprised to see her act as though she was the equal of her husband.

"It is different here in America," Toyoko said suddenly.

But Koichi didn't know the thoughts that had been skimming through Toyoko's head. Thinking that she spoke of the hot sun, he said, "I know, we have to keep the cellar dry, with fresh air, but no sun."

Toyoko let the matter go. "I'll clean out the boxes each day," she offered, wanting to say it before Koichi told her to do it.

"That's good," Koichi said. Maybe it wasn't going to be so bad having Toyoko around to help after all.

At the end of their first day, the silkworms had enough to eat but not even half the mulberry trees had been planted, the tea and sesame seeds had not been unwrapped from their bundles, and the bamboo and lacquer and wax trees lay forlornly on the ground, waiting for water and the cool dampness of the earth.

"We must hurry," the farmers urged.

"It will take time, but we will succeed," Father said.

"We need more water from the creek," Rintaro warned.

Each night after a long day's work, they spoke of all that still needed to be done. It was like running a race. They could not stop until everything was planted and watered, for if they did, they would lose the race.

Koichi worked hard at caring for the silkworms, for it was an important task that also made him a part of this great race they were having with the sun and the earth in this strange land. He and Toyoko fed them five times a day and kept their beds clean and fresh. The first thing each morning, they rushed down to the cellar and listened for the sounds of the silkworms munching noisily on the leaves. As long as they kept eating, they were alive and well, and in a month they would be ready to spin cocoons and then there would be silk to reel.

Okei and Toyoko's mother came each day to see the silkworms, and at night, Rintaro and Father and some of the others came too. Herr Schnell did not bother to go look at them but said only, "I trust you and Toyoko are taking good care of the silkworms, Koichi."

Koichi somehow couldn't tell Herr Schnell how the silkworms were growing into plump gray creatures whose munching filled the cellar with hundreds of busy sounds. Nor could he tell him that he was determined that they should be the biggest, fattest silkworms in all of America.

Herr Schnell's harsh green eyes kept the words locked inside, and Koichi could only answer, "Yes, Herr Schnell."

It was Toyoko who spoke up to her father. "You should just see them, Papa," she said eagerly. "Koichi-san and I are raising the best silkworms in the whole world."

Herr Schnell allowed a slight flicker of a smile to cross his lips. "Good," he said simply, and turned again to reading *The Sacramento Daily Union*, his moustache twitching occasionally according to how good or bad the news was.

One day about two weeks after they had arrived, Herr Schnell put on his best suit and rode into town. When he returned, he quickly gathered everyone in the front parlor.

"It is done!" he said proudly. "The land is now officially ours." And pulling the deed to the land from his pocket, he held it up for them to see. "Listen," he said, "I will read it to you."

Although most of them would not understand the words, they gathered around Herr Schnell, some sitting on chairs and some on the floor, where they felt more at home.

Herr Schnell's booming voice filled the room as he began to

read. "This indenture, made the eighteenth day of June in the year of our Lord one thousand eight hundred and sixty-nine, between Charles M. Graner of the County of El Dorado and State of California, party of the first part, and J. Henry Schnell, the party of the second part. Witnesseth: That the said party of the first part for and in consideration of the sum of five thousand dollars. . . ."

Five thousand dollars. That sounded like all the money in the world to Koichi, and he hoped Herr Schnell hadn't used up all the gold pieces in the drawstring bag. Soon Koichi didn't even try to listen for words that he knew. He stifled a yawn and studied the big Prussian's face. His moustache moved up and down with each word, and his dark eyebrows moved like two grown silkworms anxious to spin their cocoons. His nose seemed unusually large and red today, and Koichi proceeded to compare it to everyone else's nose. Toyoko's was the smallest. Koichi felt his own nose. It too was small, and not very noble.

He wished Herr Schnell would hurry, for he wanted to go down to tend to the silkworms before supper. But Herr Schnell did not stop until he reached the name of the justice who signed the deed and the time and date and place where the deed was filed.

"Now," he said, as though he had just delivered an address to Lord Matsudaira's council, "the Wakamatsu Colony is officially founded." He bowed, and everyone bowed back, and Father rose to thank him for guiding them safely to their new home.

It was decided that in commemoration of this special day, they would plant a small cedar sapling in front of the house.

"Good," Okei said with a small sigh. "That will take away the bad fortune of the willow tree." And she hurried to the kitchen to prepare some tea in celebration of the happy event.

Koichi hurried down to the cellar, with Toyoko following close behind. The moment they got there, however, Koichi knew something was wrong. The cellar was strangely quiet and there were no sounds of chewing. He peered quickly at the boxes and saw that many of the small gray bodies were lying stiff and still.

"They're dying!" he shouted.

"All of them?"

"Most of them." Koichi ran upstairs shouting, "The silkworms are dying! Something is wrong!"

Now everyone ran down with Koichi, crowding around to see what had happened. "It could be a disease," one of the farmers said, as he inspected the stiff silent creatures. "Or," another said, "it might be that the mulberry leaves were diseased."

No one was sure, but they all knew that those that still lived needed to be separated from the dead silkworms. Everyone helped and the cellar was filled with quiet activity.

"Will they all die?" Koichi asked the farmers.

They shook their heads. "It does not look good," they said.

"They would have been ready to start spinning their cocoons in two more weeks," Koichi said miserably.

One of the farmers put a hand on his shoulder. "It is too bad, Koichi-san," he said.

And Koichi knew then that by tomorrow they would probably all be dead.

A FAILURE AND A FIGHT

Koichi was the first one down in the cellar the next morning. Almost without looking, he knew what he would find in the boxes, for the cellar was strangely silent.

"Are they all dead?" a small voice asked behind him. It was Toyoko, pale and thin in her cotton kimono, her bare feet thrust hurriedly into her sandals.

Koichi looked and nodded. "They're all dead," he said.

"I wonder what we did wrong?" Toyoko asked anxiously.

It was hard to tell. Perhaps they had not cleaned the boxes often enough. Perhaps the mulberry leaves were diseased. Perhaps it was just the long journey that had made them sick. Whatever it was, it was too late to do anything now. The silkworms were dead.

Okei saw their sad faces as Koichi and Toyoko came into the kitchen.

"Even my mother's silkworms died sometimes," she said quickly. "Sometimes they just become sick and no one can help it. It's not your fault, you know. They might have died even if Herr Schnell himself was taking care of them."

Okei's words didn't help. Koichi felt as though he had let the entire colony down. He had told Herr Schnell he could take care of the silkworms and he had failed. Now he might never be trusted with another task again.

"I'm fixing a Japanese breakfast this morning," Okei said, trying to cheer him.

"No porridge or milk?"

"Rice and pickled cucumbers and tea!"

Koichi finally smiled. That would be good. Although he liked Kate Whitlow, he didn't think much of the breakfasts she had taught Okei to make. "The little ones need plenty of milk," Kate had cautioned, but neither Toyoko nor Koichi could get used to the taste of it. One morning Koichi had mooed like a cow as Toyoko sipped her cup of milk, and she had had to run to the sink to spit it out.

"You're horrid!" she had cried to Koichi.

But Father had laughed and said, "Well, well, so you two are finally becoming friends."

Friends or not, they had failed together in their first important task for the colony, and Koichi did not want to face Herr Schnell when he came down to breakfast. He was glad that Father and Rintaro came down first.

Father had only to look at Koichi's glum face to know what had happened. "Never mind," he said. "You and Toyoko did your best."

"That's right," Rintaro nodded. "That's what matters."

When Herr Schnell heard the news, he was neither angry nor upset. "I have learned that there is another man in El Dorado County who is also raising silkworms," he said. "Perhaps if we can pay enough, he would be willing to sell us some of his seed next year."

"But then they won't be Japanese silkworms," Koichi objected. "They won't be as good as ours."

Herr Schnell sucked in his breath. "Well," he said slowly, "we will just have to wait and see about that."

Koichi was surprised at the ease with which Herr Schnell had shrugged off their first failure. Didn't he even care that the silkworms they had brought so carefully from Japan had died? Didn't he care at all how hard he and Toyoko had tried to make them live?

Rintaro knew how Koichi felt.

"Never mind," he comforted. "There will be other ways you can help the colony. You'll find a way someday. You'll see. Now forget about the silkworms and come into town with me today. You too, Toyoko."

Rintaro had learned to drive the wagon to Coloma and now it was he who went each week to pick up their supplies.

Koichi had never seen Coloma. He ran outside now to help Rintaro hitch up the horses, and Toyoko climbed into the back seat just as her mother would have done. They set off down the road in a clatter of red dust, for Rintaro loved to gallop the horses even when there was no need to hurry.

They bumped along, past fruit orchards and sheep farms, past square box-like stone houses and some two-storied pillared houses. As they neared the south fork of the American River, Rintaro finally slowed down. "Well, here we are," he said. "This is Coloma." And he pointed out the sights as though he were a guide.

"See that old lumber mill over there?" he said. "That's no ordinary lumber mill. They call it Sutter's Mill and that's the very place where gold was first discovered in California. Those empty log cabins and shacks nearby are where the prospectors lived when they were looking for gold. And that's Brooks Store where they bought their supplies."

"I wish we had come then," Koichi said longingly, "when there was still lots of gold around."

"Isn't there any left at all?" Toyoko asked. "Not even some tiny little pieces someplace?"

55

Rintaro shrugged. "Could be," he said. "There're still some miners around looking. Maybe someday. . . ."

"Someday what, Rintaro?"

But Rintaro was pointing to something else. "Look to the right now, that's the hotel and the post office and the blacksmith's. And over here, that's John Little's Emporium and Captain Shannon's store, and there, that's a two-story theater right in Coloma. Imagine that!" Rintaro pointed out every building on the main street as though he had lived here all his life.

"Rintaro," Toyoko whispered plaintively. "They're all staring again." She looked down at her feet to avoid the stares of the people on the street.

Koichi, however, had grown bolder since the days when they first arrived. "Let them look," he said defiantly, and he stared straight ahead as Rintaro had taught him to do. "Next time I come to town," he said, "I'm going to wear my sword." He noticed that Rintaro was wearing his short sword thrust inside his sash and wondered if he would ever have to use it.

They came to a stop in front of a shop called Bellweather's General Store. It was sandwiched between the Gold Hill Bar and Hop Yeung's Shoe Repair Shop.

"This is where we buy our supplies," Rintaro explained, as he led the way into the crowded shop. Every inch of it seemed filled with boxes, barrels, tins and bins, and the store smelled of coffee and bacon and salt beef and tobacco.

"How do, Mr. Bellweather," Rintaro called out in his best English. Rintaro had made several trips into town and knew the shopkeeper by name. "I need flour and sugar and beans and salt," he added, to show that he had come on business.

Hiram Bellweather was a tall thin man with a shock of dark bushy hair, and a beard that flourished luxuriously on his chin. He came from behind the counter and bent to examine Koichi and Toyoko with his deep blue eyes.

"Well, so this here's the little boy and girl from the Graner place," he said, stooping from his enormous height to shake their hands.

Koichi bowed. "I am called Matsuzaka, Koichi," he said, for this seemed the only proper way to greet this giant of a shopkeeper.

Hearing Koichi, Toyoko did the same. "I am called Schnell, Toyoko," she said in a thin high voice.

The tall man grinned. "My name is Hiram Bellweather," he said very politely. Then, reaching into a half-empty candy jar, he took out a peppermint stick for each of them. "Here y'are," he said with a flourish. "Reckon this'll keep you both happy for a while."

"Thank you very . . ." Koichi began in his finest English, when there was a terrible racket at the doorway.

Two large men came spilling into the shop from the saloon next door, reeking of whiskey and tobacco. They looked Rintaro over from head to toe with unpleasant smirks twisting their mouths.

"Wal, wal, whatta we got here?" they grinned.

Then one of the men, who wore a black patch over his left eye, stepped up to Rintaro and shoved him aside.

"Your turn *after* me!" he snarled, and pounding on the counter, he demanded a tin of tobacco.

"Now hold on a minute, One-eye," Hiram Bellweather began, and then he stopped, for the second man had moved toward Rintaro with his hand on his knife.

Hiram quickly pushed the tobacco across the counter. "There's your tobacco. Now get out," he said sternly.

For a long minute, the one-eyed man and Hiram Bellweather glared at each other, neither of them sure how far the other would go.

Koichi and Toyoko had backed up toward the corner where the boots and guns and knives were kept. Koichi glanced at the nearest knife. Should he take one and lunge at the man? He had insulted Rintaro, and Koichi could see that Rintaro's hand was ready to move quickly toward his sword. If there was going to be a fight, Koichi was going to help.

Koichi edged a little closer to the knives, but before he could make another move, the one-eyed man's friend lunged at him.

"Oh no ya don't," he shouted. And grabbing Koichi's shoulder, he spun him around and knocked him to the floor. In a flash, Rintaro was on top of the man who had attacked Koichi.

"Mama! Papa! Help!" Toyoko shouted.

Quickly Hiram leaped from behind the counter and jumped on the one-eyed man. Everyone was scuffling and pushing and grunting and shouting, and for a terrible minute, Koichi thought they would all be killed. He didn't know how Rintaro did it, but he had seized the big man by the neck and, with a bloodcurdling yell, had hurled him away from Koichi and against the counter.

Hiram Bellweather, in the meantime, had given One-eye a resounding blow on the chin and sent him reeling out the door. His friend soon followed him.

"Trash!" Hiram Bellweather shouted. "Them miners is nothing but trash!"

Rintaro looked pale. "Are you all right, Koichi? Toyoko?" he asked. Then glaring out the door he muttered, "Next time I will not hold back. I will use my sword."

Hiram seemed to know what Rintaro was saying. "Wouldn't mess no more with them if I was you," he said. "They fight dirty."

Rintaro said nothing more, but Koichi knew that he hadn't finished with the one-eyed man. And the next time they met, Koichi knew the other man had better watch out.

A MYSTERIOUS PACKET

The summer days were long and hot, and the air shimmered gold in the heat of the sun.

"Does it never rain in California?" the farmers wondered anxiously. "Do the clouds never come to shield us from the eternal sun?" they asked.

The men grew brown and wiry from long days in the fields, but the plantings seemed to shrivel instead of grow green and leafy. Even the big creek that ran through their land seemed to be shrinking, for the melting mountain snows had long since stopped feeding it.

"The big creek does not give us enough water," Rintaro observed.

"But at least it gives us trout for the table," Father answered.

Father was the elder statesman of the colony. He remained calm and steady when the others grew anxious, and he tried to be encouraging. "Give the trees and plants time to grow accustomed to their new home," he said. "They will survive."

"And if they do not?"

"Then Herr Schnell will send for more from Japan. We will have a good farm one day. Do not despair."

The men listened to Father and tried to dispel their fears. They worked hard from early morning until the sun dipped beyond the hills that stretched to the west. They dug new ditches to bring more water to their fields, and they worked the soil around the plantings so they would draw water and air to grow.

It was the time of year to tap the lacquer trees, but they dared not try until the trees were securely rooted. The craftsmen were disappointed there would be no lacquer to work with this year, for Wakamatsu was famous throughout Japan for its fine lacquerware and they were eager to show their skill to the Americans. Their fingers ached to be making beautiful trays and chests and boxes instead of grasping the handle of a hoe.

When Kate Whitlow saw Mrs. Schnell's red lacquered writing box with the golden crane flying on its cover, she had exclaimed, "Why, I declare, it's fitting for a prince!" And indeed it was. The craftsman had made it especially for Lord Matsudaira, who had presented it to the Schnells on their wedding day.

Toyoko's mother had not only brought along her precious writing box, she had managed to bring her small black and gold altar as well. And because it was the only one that had been brought, it was used by everyone as a common family altar. The dead of all their families were remembered there.

Each morning and evening, Okei put a small serving of rice at the altar for their deceased ancestors and families, and Koichi tried to remember to say a prayer for his grandfather and his mother and brother whenever he rushed by on the way to the fields.

Toyoko's mother polished the altar now, making sure it was free of every bit of dust. She saw that there were fresh candles in the holders and incense in the containers.

"It is almost time for the Obon festival," she said. "We must prepare for the visit of our spirit guests."

"Will they find us way over here in America?" Toyoko asked anxiously.

"I think so," her mother answered.

But Toyoko wanted to be sure. She asked Koichi.

"Of course they'll find us," Koichi answered, but he wasn't too sure himself.

"Suppose they go to Wakamatsu and don't find us there?"

"Then they'll cross the ocean and come look for us here."

At least that was what Koichi supposed would happen. After all, the spirits of all the dead returned each year to visit their families during Obon, and surely they would not be stopped by an ocean. Koichi asked Father to be doubly sure.

"An ocean is only a drop of water in the spirit world," Father said without a moment's hesitation, "and a continent a speck of dust. They will find us, Koichi."

"And if Grandmother is waiting for them in Wakamatsu?"

"I think they will visit her first and then come here." Father smiled, pleased at the thought that they would all be united again—the dead and the living, those still in their earthly home and those who had crossed to another shore. "Yes, Koichi," he mused. "We will have a fine Obon this year."

For days before the thirteenth day of the eighth month, Okei and Toyoko's mother began cleaning the house. They swept it from top to bottom with big floppy brooms that Rintaro had bought from Mr. Bellweather, and they got on their hands and knees to scrub the floors and woodwork with hot wet cloths.

Okei prepared a small table in front of the altar and put fresh fruit and vegetables on it for their spirit guests. Wishing she had lotus root and taro and persimmon, she sent Koichi and Toyoko out to the fields and woods to collect basketfuls of blackberries and nuts.

The evening of Obon, a lamp was lighted beside the altar and the front door opened to welcome the returning spirits. The men came in early from the fields to scrub themselves in hot tubs with bags of rice bran, and everyone was in fresh cotton kimonos that smelled of sun and soap.

Just before dusk, Koichi and Toyoko went out to the front gate and prepared a small pile of dried grass and sticks. When everyone was ready, they went out to light the welcoming fire. Koichi watched it burst into a small blaze of welcome for the returning spirits and he felt once more the special peace and joy that Obon always brought.

If they had been home in Wakamatsu, there would have been welcome fires burning at every gateway, but here, no one even understood what they were doing. A wagon rumbled by as they stood at the gate, but the driver only stared curiously and rattled off leaving a trail of red dust.

There was no priest to pray for the peaceful rest of the visiting spirits, but Father struck the small gong at the altar and they all knelt beside him, bowing to the floor to welcome the spirits of the dead.

"Let us celebrate Obon in America with joy in our hearts," Father said, and they gathered at the table to eat the special Japanese dishes that the women had prepared.

It was not until after supper that Koichi noticed the small packet of paper on the special table set before the altar. It was folded carefully, like a packet of medicinal herbs that Grandmother opened when one of them was ill. Koichi picked it up and sniffed, but it smelled of nothing at all. He put it down quickly as Toyoko approached.

"Come outside and help me catch a cicada," she urged. Surrounded by their insistent buzzing, she was determined to catch one and cage it as she used to do back home. Every evening she went out with a small basket, and if there was nothing better to do, Koichi went with her. Tonight, however, he had something else on his mind and he didn't want Toyoko around.

"You go by yourself," he said, adding, "You'd better hurry or it'll be time for you to go to bed."

He waited until she had skipped happily from the room and then picked up the small packet again. He looked around quickly and saw that all the men were outside on the porch, smoking their pipes and speaking of what Japan must be like now under the Emperor's rule. Okei and Toyoko's mother were still washing dishes in the tub of soapy water in the kitchen.

Koichi unfolded the paper packet carefully, and gasped when he saw what was inside. "Gold!" he murmured. It was a pinch of gold dust and he guessed it must have been Rintaro who put it there as a special gift to their spirit guests.

Koichi hurried to the porch, but Rintaro was not there. He walked around the house, past the well and past the vegetable garden Okei had begun. He walked toward the knoll where Okei went each evening to watch the sunset and to look toward home. Halfway up the knoll, sitting under a low oak tree was Rintaro enjoying his solitude and a bottle of whiskey.

"*Yah*, Koichi. Come sit with me," he called out in friendly fashion.

"Was it you who put it on the table?" Koichi asked, flopping down beside Rintaro on the dry weeds.

Rintaro took a swallow of whiskey, wiped his mouth and sighed happily. "What?" he asked.

"The gold dust. Was it you?"

Rintaro grinned. "I put it there," he admitted. "Was it not a fine gift for the spirit guests?"

"I've never seen such a fine gift," Koichi said. "Where did you get it? Did someone give it to you?"

"No."

"You found it yourself?"

"In a manner of speaking. I had a little help."

"From Mr. Bellweather?"

"No, another friend. . . . He is an Indian."

"An Indian!" Koichi had heard Herr Schnell speak of an Indian village not far from Gold Hill. "You know a real Indian?" he asked now, greatly impressed.

"Well, we do not speak much, for neither of us knows the other's tongue," Rintaro explained, "but one day he showed me how to catch fish with a net instead of a pole."

"And . . . ?" Koichi urged impatiently as Rintaro took another swallow from his bottle.

"And one day he led me up the big creek, almost to his village, and showed me how to pan for gold. I gave him the trout I caught that day in exchange," Rintaro said expansively.

Koichi was on his feet now. "Take me with you," he begged. "Show me where you found the gold and how you catch fish with a net. Show me the Indian."

Rintaro was leaning against the tree trunk now, his eyes closed and a faint smile still on his face. "All in good time, Koichi-san," he said sleepily. "All in good time."

ENCOUNTER AT
THE CREEK

The endless days of hot dry sun marched on and on, like a parade of brown soldiers that would never come to a halt. Now it was already the ninth month of the year, and still each long day continued to be bathed in the brilliant heat of the sun.

Although they worried about the drying of the fields, Okei and Toyoko's mother delighted in the way the laundry dried. Every day they boiled huge tubs of hot water, filled them with soap that Kate Whitlow helped them make, and poked and prodded the clothes like huge pots of stew to get them clean. Ignoring the clothesline that Thomas Whitlow had strung up for them, they threaded bamboo poles through the sleeves and hung the kimonos up on forked poles, so they looked like bodiless souls flapping listlessly in the sun.

Sitting in the yard under a poplar tree, carving a wooden whistle for himself, Koichi thought the clothes looked like a row of trapped ghosts, arms outstretched, unable to flee from their bamboo captors. He watched now as Okei hung out the last of her morning's wash. She wiped her forehead with her arm and glanced over at Koichi.

"Why aren't you out weeding with the others?" she asked. "The farmers say the weeds are the only healthy things on our farm. They say they grow back as fast as they're pulled out."

"I don't feel like weeding," Koichi said. "It makes my back ache."

"And your father permitted you to stay home?"

"I didn't ask him."

"*Mah!*" Okei was shocked. "That doesn't sound at all like you, Koichi-san," she reflected.

"I'm tired of being a farmer."

Okei looked distressed. "You mustn't speak like that," she said with a troubled frown. "That is our task here. To start a fine farm."

Koichi didn't know himself just what had come over him. He knew as well as Okei why they were there. And he knew too that he should be loyal to his father as well as to the whole colony. It was just that it was so hard to live and work like a farmer and still think the thoughts of a samurai. It was not only Koichi who felt the strain. The others felt it too, although no one dared speak the thoughts that troubled their lonely hours.

Koichi couldn't put into words all that was going on inside his head. He just knew that he didn't want to spend another day bending in the hot sun, digging at the endless weeds. He knew, however, that he owed Okei an explanation, and not being able to give one, he offered to go catch her a fish for supper.

"Do you want me to?" he asked.

"No, not today," Okei answered. "Rintaro said he would catch some fish for me this afternoon. He says he has found a special place where he can always find fish."

Koichi sat up. "He has? Where?"

"He does not tell me such things," Okei said simply. "He only told me that a friend had shown him the place."

"What friend? An Indian?"

"He did not say, Koichi-san."

Koichi knew that he had to go with Rintaro when he went fishing that afternoon. He stood up quickly, put away his half-finished whistle and headed toward the fields. He would help Rintaro weed his patch of land and they could finish early and go on up to the creek.

"Koichi-san," Toyoko called from the porch as Koichi streaked by. "Do you have a poem ready for the moon viewing tonight?"

She flung the question at him as though it was the only important thing in the whole world.

Koichi shook his head. "I can't write poems until I see the moon," he said, although, of course, this wasn't true. "I'll think of one tonight."

"You'd better," Toyoko warned, "because everyone is going to have a poem ready, and the one with the best poem gets an extra sweet cake."

Koichi nodded as he tied on his straw hat. Toyoko's words were filtering into his head, but all he could think about was going fishing with Rintaro and his Indian friend.

They set off together shortly after the afternoon break for tea, walking quickly toward the upper boundary of their land. Koichi could feel the dry weeds tickle his legs and the warmth of the dirt oozing into the crevices between his toes. They swept past the chaparral, past clumps of scrub oak and buckeye, and made their way through the manzanitas toward the big creek. Koichi saw that Rintaro had not brought his fishing pole, but carried only his sword and a faded sack hung over his shoulder.

Rintaro slowed his pace as they approached the creek, and he thrust his head forward, as though by doing that he could see through the trees.

It was Koichi who saw the Indian first. He was a tall black-haired bronze-colored man, wearing a necklace of beads and feathers and a brief animal skin slung about his hips. Koichi had never seen a more beautiful human being. His body rippled with firm muscles, his back was as straight as a spear, and his swift graceful movements were like those of a deer.

"Maidu-san!" Rintaro called out when he saw him.

When he had first met the Indian, the man had pointed to himself and said, "Me, Maidu," and Rintaro, not knowing that this was his tribe, had thought it was his name.

"Me, Rintaro," he had answered proudly, and the Indian had allowed him to watch as he caught his fish, not with a pole but with a net or a spear.

The Maidu looked hard now at Koichi. There was no hatred in his eyes, however, only curiosity. Koichi bowed. The Indian nodded, and then turning, quickly dipped his net into the flowing water and came up with a thrashing, splashing silvery trout. He took it from the net and gave it to Koichi.

Koichi grinned. He accepted the fish with both hands, and raised it toward his forehead to show his thanks. He wished he had something to give to the Indian in return, and offered him his bamboo pole.

The Indian, however, did not take it and held out his own net for Koichi to try. Koichi waded out into the water, waited quietly until he saw a fish, and then dipped quickly as the Indian had done. The net struck the water with a splash, and the fish slithered away. Koichi had done nothing but cover himself with water. The Indian indicated with a wave of the hand that he should try again.

"Get the net into the water like an arrow," Rintaro advised. "Quick and quiet!"

Koichi tried again and again, but the fish were too fast for him. He wanted to stay and try until he actually caught a fish, but Rintaro had other plans. He drew the Indian aside, and rubbing his fingers to indicate gold dust, he said, "Show me place, find gold."

The Indian nodded. "Come, follow," he said motioning, and he set out so quickly that Koichi had to run to keep up.

The Indian moved like an animal, swiftly and silently, and he did not have to look back to know that Rintaro and Koichi were following him. He continued through the pine and white alders and then moved up a rocky path that followed the bend of the creek. There were boulders along the creek now, and the water tumbling over the rocks had a loud and urgent sound.

"Is he taking us to a gold mine?" Koichi asked breathlessly.

"Not a mine," Rintaro answered, "just a place upstream where there are still a few gold fragments."

Gold! The very word gripped Koichi with excitement. How wonderful it would be to march home triumphantly with a fistful of gold dust. It would make up for the silkworms that had died and for the days when he hated being a farmer and didn't work as hard as he should. It would make up for a lot of things, and Father and Herr Schnell wouldn't have to worry so much about not having any tea or silk to sell.

When the Indian came to the right spot, he stopped and pointed. Rintaro drew out an old tin pan from his sack and waded into the water close to the boulders. He peered into the back eddies, where the restless water had deposited some fragments of gold, and submerged the pan in the water. Filling it with dirt, he swished it back and forth, spilling out the lighter dirt and pebbles and sand. Then he held the pan out for Koichi to see, and there at the bottom glittered a few small pieces of gold.

"Gold! It really is gold!" Koichi shouted, scarcely able to contain himself. He thrust his hand into the water, sweeping it around to see if he couldn't discover some himself. All he did, however, was stir up the dirt so he could see nothing.

"Now don't scrape around just anyplace," Rintaro cautioned. "What you have to do is pan 'selected dirt.' "

He held the pan toward Koichi now, knowing that he was about to perish for wanting to try. "Here," he said, "stand right here and do as I did."

Koichi bent eagerly to his task and in the third panful found his first bit of gold. "Rintaro, look! I've found some," he shouted. "We're going to get rich!"

He had just bent to try again when he heard someone coming up the path. The Indian stiffened and gripped his spear. "Someone come," he said quietly.

Rintaro quickly took the pan from Koichi and tried to hide it behind one of the boulders. He didn't want everyone in Gold Hill to know there was gold here. But it was too late. They had already been seen, and by the one person in all of Coloma they wanted most to avoid. It was the one-eyed man.

He knew immediately what they were doing. "So, ya found some gold didja?" he sneered. "Wal, you kin just clear right on outta here. Ain't no brown or red man gonna pan fer no gold till us whites is finished with a place."

Rintaro glared at him, his eyes dark with hate, but he said nothing.

The one-eyed man went on. "Ain't no brown man can file claims here and ain't none can go to no schools either." He seemed to add the last for Koichi's benefit, although it was something Koichi had already discovered long ago. "If there's gold here, I'm claimin' it," he shouted. "So clear out!"

That was all Rintaro was going to stand for. Before the Indian could come to his side, or before Koichi could even think what to do, Rintaro had drawn his sword and lunged at One-eye. They both rolled over and over on the ground, thrashing and battering at each other. One-eye was bigger, but Rintaro knew better how to use his strength.

"Watch out!" Koichi shouted, as he saw One-eye reach for his knife.

The Indian moved closer, but he did not interfere. He seemed to know that this was something Rintaro had to settle for himself, and Koichi knew that too. The two men grunted and grappled and now One-eye had his knife in his hand too. It was a matter of who could strike first.

Koichi stepped closer. He could see that Rintaro was not trying to kill the man, but One-eye's knife was perilously close to Rintaro's throat. Koichi remembered what Hiram Bellweather had said.

"Rintaro!" he shouted again. "Be careful!"

But now Rintaro struck. Blood spurted from One-eye's right arm and he dropped his knife to the ground, howling in pain. Rintaro stopped fighting and stood up. "*You* get out!" he shouted at One-eye.

Koichi had never seen such anger and hatred as he saw on One-eye's face. He was shouting words that Koichi had never heard before and couldn't understand. Finally, he backed away, shouting, "Yer gonna pay for this! You'll see! Yer gonna wish you never set foot in this here land, the whole lot of ya!"

He tried to reach for his gun, but his right hand was useless. He turned then and staggered back down the path, still shouting angrily as he left.

The Indian watched him go, murmuring, "That one have evil heart."

Rintaro sat panting on a boulder and nodded in agreement. "Maybe I should have killed," he said. "Maybe better dead."

Then, turning to Koichi, he said, "Well, that is the end of our gold."

"He'll come back and take it all?"

Rintaro nodded. "It is as he said. The white man takes first, and if anything is left, then the brown man and red man can have it."

Koichi had never seen Rintaro look so angry. "We had better go now," he said, "before he comes back with his friends. This time they will use their guns."

Putting his pan back into his sack, he urged Koichi to hurry along, and Koichi knew they would not be panning for gold again. He also had a terrible feeling that One-eye wasn't finished with Rintaro yet.

HIRAM'S PROMISE

"Full moon
at Gold Hill,
small comfort
to my longing heart."

Okei flushed with embarrassment as she recited her own
haiku, and she looked down at the hands she twisted in her
lap.

"That was very good, Okei," Koichi's father said quickly.
"Very good indeed."

They were all sitting on the front porch, watching the full
moon rise over the cluster of trees. It was much like the moon
viewings they used to have at their old house near the castle,
Koichi thought, only here there were no sweet rice-flour cakes.
The women had done their best, but all they could make were
sweet cakes of crushed lima beans and sugar. Koichi wished
they could hurry with the poems and get on with the tea and
cakes.

"You're next," Toyoko said to him now. "Hurry and say
yours and then Rintaro will, and then we can have our tea."
Toyoko looked expectantly at Koichi, her hands folded neatly
in her lap.

Koichi looked up at the moon and cleared his throat. He hadn't a single solitary poem in his head, but he tried now to think of something that would express not only his manliness, but a love for the world of nature. He knew that a good samurai not only excelled in the arts of war, but in all the arts, being at ease in the courts of the lord as well as on the battlefield.

Koichi sniffed and rubbed his nose. "White cloud in the sky," he began, only now forming the words he was supposed to have given thought to all day. "Are you a brave Aizu warrior . . . or only our shattered castle?"

Koichi didn't dare look up. His poem did not show any great depth of thought, but Toyoko clapped her hands anyway.

"That was good," she said. "It was sad because you thought of home and the clan and, well, it was nice, Koichi-san."

She could think of nothing more to say of it and glanced now at Rintaro. "It's your turn, Rintaro," she said. "You're the very last."

Rintaro did not look at any of them as he spoke, but turned toward the black shadowy trees beyond the road, his eyes just as forbidding.

"Blood on my blade,
hate in my heart.
My hand rests lightly
on my sword."

Rintaro blurted out the words, his voice sharp. Everyone was startled by the sudden anger in Rintaro's haiku and no one knew quite what to make of it. Only Koichi knew why Rintaro spoke as he did. Only Koichi knew what had happened up at the creek with the one-eyed man. Koichi glanced at Rintaro now, wondering what had made him spill out his anger for everyone to see.

Almost as suddenly as the anger had burst out, however, it

seemed to melt away. Rintaro looked at the startled faces around him and grinned. "It is nothing, my friends," he said. "It was the poem of a warrior. You see, I was dreaming I was a samurai in Wakamatsu, that's all." He glanced at the sweet cakes and murmured, "Well, Toyo-chan, who is to win the extra sweet?"

Forgetting the strange fear that crept through her as she listened to Rintaro's haiku, Toyoko picked up the tray of sweets.

"I choose Okei's," she said. "I liked Okei's best." And she hurried to present the extra sweet to the still-blushing Okei.

Although the others were satisfied with Rintaro's explanation, he had not fooled Koichi's father. When the moon had risen beyond the roof and the sweet cakes had been eaten, Father took Rintaro aside.

"Have you done something you should not?" he asked in a low voice. "Whose blood is on your blade?"

But Rintaro was not going to tell him. "It is nothing," he said quickly. "You have enough to worry about. Do not worry about me. It is nothing."

Koichi's father looked at him gravely. "Take care not to make enemies in this land," he warned. "In this country, if you are an Oriental, you have already lost half the battle before it is begun. Did you not know that, Rintaro?"

"Yes, I know."

"Then do not forget it," Father reminded him. "And Rintaro. . . ."

"Yes?"

"Be careful."

"I will."

Hiram Bellweather said the same thing to Rintaro the next time he saw him at the shop. "Better watch out for that scoundrel," he warned. "Sounded to me like he's out to get you."

Koichi shuffled his feet uncomfortably at the thought. "I'll help Rintaro fight," he said. "I'm a good fighter."

But Hiram quickly told Koichi to shush up. "Now the both of you, listen," he said urgently. "There's a sheriff in this here town to take care of the likes of One-eye. Don't try nothing yourselves or you might just end up ten feet under. Do you follow me?"

"I follow," Rintaro nodded obediently, although Koichi was quite sure he hadn't really understood everything Hiram had said.

When Hiram got excited, he spoke in great gusts of words, and neither Rintaro nor Koichi knew what in the world he was talking about. It was like the times when he got to talking about the early days. Hiram was happiest when he talked of the days when the veins of gold ran rich and heavy in the land, and Coloma was jammed with people who came flooding to California from every state in the union. He loved to tell the story of how he came to California, and Koichi asked him about it whenever he had a chance.

"It was a long time ago," Hiram would begin, his mind and heart drifting back to those exciting times. "Everybody in this here country had gold fever bad, and I was one of them. I hitched up with an ox team starting out from Illinois where I come from. Had to drive the team part way myself and darn near drove 'em straight into a mud bank. We almost lost the wagon that day," he would say, laughing. "Finally, we begun running out of grub and me and a buddy, we left the train with only one blanket, six dollars and one pancake from the cook between us. First night out, them howling wolves like to scared us to death when they come after all them dead horses and mules strung out on the trail along with the junk people kept throwing out to lighten their loads. Well, we kept going till we come to a trading post where we paid one dollar and twenty-five cents just for a gallon of warm water and a handful of soda crackers."

At this point, Hiram always looked to his listeners for a sympathetic groan, and Koichi always remembered to give it to him.

"Much money just for water and crackers," he would say.

And Hiram would nod. "It sure was. Long about that time, we was running out of money, and if a wagon train hadn't taken us in, we might of never got out here."

"And then you came and found lots and lots of gold?" Koichi would ask.

"First off, I worked in a brickyard in Sacramento to earn enough to get to Coloma. Then, I dug for gold night and day, like a crazy fool. I staked me a claim up the river and used everything from my fingers to spoons to iron bars to dig that gold out of all them cracks and crevices."

This was the part Koichi liked best, the part about finding the gold, and he listened especially hard, trying to catch every word.

"Why, I reckon all them miners and prospectors turned up so much earth in them hills and ravines, they must of moved whole hills and mountainsides," Hiram would say. "There was so much gold in this earth then, some men made fortunes overnight, and sometimes spent 'em in a day. I finally got me a rocker to speed up my work 'fore the gold was all gone."

"And that's how you got that bottle full of gold dust?" Koichi asked.

Just once, Hiram had gone out behind his shop and dug up the bottle of gold dust he kept buried at the foot of the pine tree out back. He had never shown it to anyone before, but he got it out for Koichi to see.

"That's cause you're sorta special," he explained.

"Special?"

"Yup, you're still a boy on the outside, but you're almost a man inside. I can't just rightly put my finger on why, but I can tell. Ain't that so, Rintaro?"

79

Rintaro nodded. "That's so," he agreed. "Koichi, my special friend."

"Mine too," Hiram said, and in a burst of goodwill, the three of them had shaken hands. Koichi had never felt so proud in his life. He wished that one day Herr Schnell would think as well of him, but he was afraid he never would.

The other part of Hiram's story that Koichi liked hearing was about the fights and killings and hangings. There used to be so many, Hiram told them, that men dealt out their own justice and Placerville was known then as Hangtown because of all the hangings that took place at an old oak tree on the edge of town.

Koichi told Hiram he'd like to see that tree someday. There were probably all kinds of ghosts and spirits still wafting around if so many men died there.

Hiram's face lit up. "You like spirits and ghosts?" he asked. "I'll take you to an Indian burning. They got enough spirits around one of them to keep you happy for the rest of your days."

"You'll take me?" Koichi asked.

"Sure."

"When?"

"Any day now they'll have one. It's always in the fall of the year."

Koichi didn't let Hiram forget. Each time he went to the shop, he asked him when it would be, and one day at last, Hiram said, "There'll be one tonight. Be ready after supper."

DANGER AT THE BURNING

They went in Hiram Bellweather's old wagon immediately after supper, the horses clopping gently on the dirt road that followed the curve of the hill. There were other wagons on their way to the burning, and some men on horseback as well. It was as though everyone were going to a carnival to have a good time instead of going to observe a ritual for the dead.

When they reached the burning grounds, it was almost time for the big fire to be lighted in the center. All around it stood long poles over twenty feet high, some laden with shirts, others with dresses or bear hides or raccoon skins or caps, and around the bases of the poles were large baskets filled with such food as flour, acorns, dried meat, fish and pine nuts.

"Those are gifts for the dead," Hiram explained, "all them clothing and provisions. They burn 'em up and send 'em up in smoke to the spirit world—to all their dead relations." He gestured with his hands to show how the smoke took the gifts to the heavens.

Koichi was amazed. There seemed to be enough food and clothing there to keep their small colony fed and clothed for over a year. "Burned!" he said again in amazement. "All that?"

Rintaro shook his head at the sight. "Our way simpler," he said to Hiram. "We give little food every day at family altar for dead relatives."

Rintaro was right, Koichi thought. It seemed strange that the Indian spirits had to wait all year for just one feast. He looked around and saw Indians coming and going quietly all around. They were putting out the small bonfires where they had cooked their meals and were moving closer now toward the big bonfire. Hiram said they had gathered from miles around. If they noticed the strange white men at the fringe of their circle, they paid no attention to them or to Rintaro and Koichi.

It was time now to light the large fire in the center of the circle and a chief rose to speak to the Indians. His strange words sounded like the call of an unknown animal. It was like the wind in the trees and like the call of wild birds in flight. And when he finished, he began to wail. It was a long low moan that grew louder and higher, and before long, the others joined in.

Koichi shuddered at the eerie unearthly sound that seemed to hold the sadness of all the world in it. It made him think of the desolation of Wakamatsu after the battle, and it made him remember the stiff lifeless body of his brother. Koichi understood how the Indians felt. In those bitter days after the defeat, he had wanted to wail too. He thought now their cries must surely be reaching the spirit world to awaken the dead.

The chief threw some nuts and acorns and dried fish into the fire, and from time to time, others would approach the fire and throw in bits of food or other offerings.

"When do they burn the gifts on the poles?" Koichi asked.

"Long about dawn."

"They wail all night then?"

Hiram nodded. "Pretty near. It's a good long cry, all right. We won't stay till the end."

Huddled in the shadows of the great circle of Indians, they watched the great fire leap higher and higher, and the strange acrid smell of the burnt offerings began to fill the air. It was dark now and the air grew cold. Koichi longed to creep closer to the big fire, not only to feel its warmth, but to have a closer look at what was going on. He glanced at Rintaro and Hiram. They were talking in low voices, their heads bent close. Perhaps they were talking of gold or the price of flour and tobacco. Or perhaps they were talking about the wives they both one day hoped to find. Whatever it was, Koichi knew neither would miss him if he left.

Koichi moved off quietly and quickly, like an Indian. He walked softly around the shadowy edge of the wailing circle and joined in the wailing. Here and there, he saw clumps of white men talking and watching, many of them lifting bottles of whiskey to their mouths, as they might when watching an entertainment. Although he looked, Koichi stayed away from them.

Then, suddenly, he saw him. It was One-eye, standing alone, a wide-brimmed felt hat jammed on his head, lifting a bottle of whiskey to his lips. Koichi moved quickly behind a tree and watched to see what One-eye was going to do. From the way he looked around, Koichi had an idea that he was looking for somebody. Was he looking for Rintaro and Hiram? Perhaps he had heard Hiram talk of bringing Rintaro to the burning. Koichi was suddenly filled with a sense of danger. Something told him that he must be watchful—that he had to watch out for Rintaro.

One-eye began to move around the fringe of the circle now, and Koichi followed him, as silent and quick as a fox. One-eye dropped his empty bottle and his right hand moved toward his gun. He was looking for somebody, and he was planning to use his gun. He wasn't watching the Indians, but looked instead at every cluster of white men who stood watching. He moved

stealthily in and out among them, and then he stopped. He had spotted Hiram and Rintaro. Koichi had guessed right.

There wasn't time to run and warn Rintaro, for One-eye would see him first. There was no use shouting, for no one could hear him over the wailing. There was only one thing to do. When One-eye drew his gun, Koichi would jump on him. He would knock the gun from his hand and maybe if it went off, the sound would attract Rintaro's attention.

Koichi was ready to spring as One-eye moved in close to get into a good position. Koichi held his breath, wishing he had his samurai sword with him. Then, just as One-eye drew, he charged with a loud cry and leaped on One-eye like a wild coyote.

"*Yai!* You miserable no-good enemy!" Koichi shouted.

One-eye was caught so completely off guard that he dropped his gun, but it did not go off. Koichi struggled with every ounce of strength he had in his body to push One-eye to the ground. But it was Koichi who got pushed to the ground instead. One-eye put a booted foot firmly on his stomach and shouted, "So, you wanna get in on the fight too, do ya? Wal, all right, I'll teach ya a lesson ya won't fergit!"

Koichi fought like a wounded tiger. "Let go!" he shouted. He tried to bite One-eye's leg, but all he got was a mouthful of his dirty boot.

"Rintaro! Help! *Tasukete!*" he shouted with all his strength, but the wailing drowned out his voice. He grabbed One-eye's leg and clung to it like a leech. Just when Koichi thought it was he who would be killed instead of Rintaro, he heard a voice.

"Take foot off boy!" It was a deep voice that rang with authority, and Koichi felt the boot removed. He leaped to his feet and saw that it was Rintaro's Indian friend.

"Maidu-san!" Koichi shouted. He was never so glad to see anyone in all his life.

The Indian, however, wasn't ready to talk to Koichi yet. "Get out!" he said firmly to One-eye, pointing toward the road. They stood glaring at each other for a long time and One-eye did not move.

"My people . . . our burning . . . not for white man. . . . Go!" The Indian summoned every word of English he knew. And then, he raised his spear and took a step toward One-eye. With that, the one-eyed man began to back away.

Twice now, he had been humbled. Once by Rintaro, and now by the Maidu Indian. Koichi saw the hatred and anger that twisted the white man's face as he spat at the Indian. Koichi knew it was meant for him as well.

One-eye turned then and slunk off into the shadows, and Koichi knew now that he was only a bully and a coward. He only dared shoot at Rintaro from the shadows, hidden and unseen. He dared fight with Koichi because he was unarmed and half his size. Confronted by Rintaro, he had fought and lost. Confronted by the Maidu Indian, he could only spit and slink away. Koichi knew then that he was no longer afraid of the one-eyed man.

He turned to thank the Indian. "Maidu-san," he began. But the Indian only motioned to him and led him back toward Rintaro and Hiram. Although they had not seen the Indian, he had known they were there all along. He had been looking out for them.

In a great outpouring of words, Koichi told Rintaro how One-eye had almost killed him, how Koichi had stopped One-eye, and then how the Indian had saved him in turn.

Rintaro shook his head in disbelief. "That scoundrel is not going to stop until he settles the score with me," he said wearily. "Koichi, thank you for saving my life."

Hiram sat beside them, not understanding the torrent of Japanese words. "Don't you wander off by yourself again, boy," he said to Koichi. "Never know what them Indians might do to you."

Koichi knew, however, that it was not the Indians he had to worry about. He wanted to tell Hiram what the Maidu had done for him, but it was too difficult to tell in English. He tried once more to thank the Indian, but now he had vanished into the shadows and melted back into the circle of his people. Koichi was glad he had not told Hiram to leave even though he was a white man too.

Rintaro looked troubled. "If I do not go away," he said more to himself than to Koichi, "that evil-hearted man will make trouble for the whole colony. I know it. He is not finished yet."

"But he's only a coward," Koichi said. "He's a coward and a bully. I'm not afraid of him anymore."

Rintaro sat quietly, his chin on his fists, listening to the wailing that swirled around them like wisps of smoke.

"The trouble with cowards," he said slowly, "is that they will not fight in the open. It is as Hiram Bellweather once said. He will fight dirty, and then it may not be only I who suffers."

There was nothing Koichi could say to that. He knew Rintaro was right.

A TIME OF HOPE

For a long time after the night of the burning, Koichi felt uneasy about One-eye. It was like having something left dangling and half finished, for both he and Rintaro knew that One-eye would not give up. It was almost worse than waiting for enemy warriors to strike. At least, if one expected the enemy, the castle could be fortified, the mountain passes guarded and the arms made ready. But what could they do to protect themselves against One-eye? He could turn up anywhere, anytime, and most likely he would approach from the rear.

Koichi worried too about Rintaro's leaving. "He'd do something hateful anyway, even if you left," he argued, trying to get Rintaro to stay.

But Rintaro didn't think so. "No, I am the one who cut him with my sword. He must do something to me to make good his name again. Don't you see? It would be better for you and for everybody in the colony if I left."

"Where would you go?"

"Hiram told me they need carpenters in many neighboring towns. He said I could go to Placerville or Folsom or even Shingle Springs and find a job anytime," Rintaro explained. "And then, too, I could make some money that way."

There was nothing much Koichi could say to that, for Rintaro certainly wasn't making any money here on the farm. No one was. Although the rains finally came in great sweeping gusts to flood their thirsty fields, it was really too late to help their trees or plants very much. They stood in the fields like scarecrows, gaunt and lifeless, looking only from a distance like living, growing things.

Koichi soon discovered that it was not only Rintaro who was thinking of leaving. One of the craftsmen left to work for a blacksmith at Mormon Island and the other went to work for a shoe repair shop in Michigan Flat. The other carpenter found work on a house going up in Pilot Hill, and even one of the farmers spoke of going to another farm or ranch to get some work.

At last, one day, Rintaro packed his belongings and told Father he was going to help build a house in Folsom. "I'll come back when you need me," he said. "When the new plantings come in the spring, I'll come to help in the fields."

"You won't be back until then?" Koichi asked dismally.

"Oh, I'll come back for visits before then," Rintaro reassured him. "I shall surely come back for the New Year celebration, and Hiram Bellweather tells me that the Americans celebrate a holiday called Christmas before that. I shall be back soon." And with a cheerful grin, Rintaro was gone.

After he left, it was Father and Koichi who went to town in the wagon for supplies, for Herr Schnell was rarely at home these days. He traveled to Sacramento and to Placerville and sometimes even to San Francisco to make plans for the marketing of their tea and silk. He was still full of fine plans and much talk, but now no one paid much attention to what he said.

Koichi was glad that Father was getting to know Hiram Bellweather.

"Your papa's a real fine gentleman, Koichi," Hiram said to him. "I can tell, he's one fine man."

And Father said of Hiram, "He's a man of good heart and strong principles. I am glad he is your friend."

One day when Hiram saw that Father did not have enough coins in his purse to pay for the beans and the rice, he quickly offered to sell to them on credit.

"I trust all of you," he said. "You pay me when you can. It's all right."

"I am very grateful," Father said, bowing.

Koichi knew it was the first time in his life that Father had not been able to pay for his food and found it necessary to rely on the kindness of a merchant to put food into his mouth. Koichi knew that Father was embarrassed, just as he was when Kate Whitlow had brought Koichi some of her husband's old shirts and pants so they could be cut down for him to wear.

"They'll be warmer than what he's got on," she said gently, "and nice for wintertime."

Father told her that Toyoko's mother was knitting sweaters for both children, but he accepted Kate's gifts with thanks. The next time they went to Hiram's shop, however, he exchanged the last of his Japanese gold pieces for a wool cap and socks and mittens for Koichi.

"There are still a few things I can do for you, Koichi," he had said sadly.

The night after Hiram had given them credit, Koichi saw Father take out one of his swords and polish it carefully with a soft silk cloth.

"Are you going to wear your swords again, Father?" Koichi asked, brightening. It would be good to see Father dressed again as a samurai should, rather than in the shabby makeshift clothes he wore in the fields.

Father shook his head. "The day of the warrior is over, Koichi," he said. "Even in Japan there is no need now for weapons."

"Then why are you polishing your sword?"

"Because I am going to . . . well, because I do not want it to rust."

Koichi knew Father wasn't telling him everything, but he knew, too, that he had said as much as he was going to. "Go to bed now, Koichi," Father said, without looking up from his sword.

The next day Father went to Coloma alone.

"He didn't even ask if we wanted to go with him," Toyoko said, sucking her thumb as she did when something upset her. "He always asks, even if I don't want to go. He didn't even ask if I wanted a sweet or some ribbon from the shop. He always asks," she said again.

"He didn't ask me either," Koichi said. And that was even more strange, for until now Father had never gone to town without him.

When Father came home, he had a big load of supplies. There was rice and a tub of soy sauce, beans, salt beef and bacon, which they had learned to eat, and large bags of sugar and salt.

"Mah," Okei exclaimed happily. "How nice it will be to have the cupboards full again."

"We had enough money for all this?" Toyoko's mother asked wonderingly. "My husband said that. . . ." She exchanged a quick glance with Father and stopped.

Suddenly Koichi knew what it was all about. He raced up the stairs and looked in Father's closet where he kept his samurai swords. It was just as he guessed. Now there was only one. Father had sold his precious sword to help them stay alive, and he had not said a word to anyone.

By December there was a sprinkling of snow on the ground like sugar icing on a cake. It was not like the heavy winter snows of Wakamatsu, and Koichi often looked at the snow-covered peaks of the Sierra Nevada rising majestically beyond the low hills that surrounded them and wished he could be up there knee-deep in snow, building a snow fort as he used to at home.

"It will soon be the holiday called Christmas," Toyoko said eagerly.

"Are we going to celebrate it too?" Koichi asked.

"Mama said we would because now we are in America. The Americans close their shops and have feasts and decorate their houses with evergreens and red berries. And best of all," Toyoko added, her eyes wide with excitement, "they give each other presents."

Toyoko paused a moment and then asked quickly, "What present would you like to have, Koichi-san? I mean if you could have anything in the world that you wanted? And no fair saying you want to go home to Wakamatsu. I don't mean that kind of present."

Koichi did not have to think for long. "A big sack of gold," he said promptly.

Toyoko frowned at Koichi. "But that's no fun," she mused. "I meant something like a kite, or a new bow and arrow, or a flute . . . something you really want."

"But I really want a sack of gold," Koichi repeated. "If I had that, I could buy anything in the world I wanted at Mr. Bellweather's shop. I could buy a bone-handled hunting knife or a gun or anything . . . I could even buy back Father's sword."

Toyoko's eyes widened. "Is that where your father's sword is now, at Mr. Bellweather's shop?"

Koichi nodded. "I think so."

Toyoko frowned and tired of her little game. "I thought we were talking about Christmas and now we're talking about not having enough money again."

It seemed these days that whenever the adults got together the talk turned to money. There was never enough, and little

hope that any would be coming in. It was a dreary prospect and made Koichi long to go off somewhere to work as Rintaro was doing. If only he could find a gold mine, he thought. If only there was something he could do to help.

On Christmas morning Rintaro came home, beaming and laden with candy for everyone, a small pocket knife for Koichi and a red hair-ribbon for Toyoko. Thomas and Kate Whitlow came to call with spicy gingerbread still warm from the oven and frosted cookies in the shape of Christmas trees and snowmen.

Hiram Bellweather came bundled in a greatcoat and scarf, leading a dancing bear on a chain. "See what I brung to show you," he shouted gaily, full of good spirits that had come both from a bottle and from closing up his shop for the holidays. And before he left, he pulled out a bag of horehound drops and peppermint sticks for Toyoko and Koichi and left a sack of sugar on the kitchen table.

Christmas was nice, but New Year's was even better, for that was the big holiday in Japan. All the men came home to Gold Hill from their jobs in other villages and towns, and the old house was filled again with talk and laughter.

For days the women had been scrubbing and cleaning the house as they had for Obon, and now they broiled trout and salmon from the streams and made rice balls sprinkled with sesame seed and cooked all the delicious Japanese dishes they could from the vegetables in the garden. They decorated the front entrance with branches of pine and bamboo, and on New Year's morning, everyone put on his best kimono and they all looked once more as they had on the morning they had landed in America.

"From this new year—the Year of the Horse—I assure you all will go better," Herr Schnell said enthusiastically. "The

94

new plants and seedlings I sent for will soon come from Japan. The winter snows will fill the big creek and streams, and there will be enough water to irrigate our fields. We have learned from the past, and this year, we will do better."

They were words of hope, and they all felt cheered, and when Rintaro sang the folk songs from their old home, they all sang with him. Okei, dressed in her best kimono, her eyes sparkling, her cheeks flushed, danced for them, looking like the doll in the glass case that Grandmother used to keep in her room.

As they all gathered together again, it seemed a time of real happiness and hope.

"It *will* be a good year," Father said, as though he was determined to make it so by saying the words.

"It will," they all agreed. "It surely will."

And at the time, neither Koichi nor Rintaro had even one small thought of One-eye and his evil schemes.

ANOTHER FRIEND GONE

"They've come! The plants have come from Japan!" It was Herr Schnell's booming voice echoing through the house.

Everyone rushed outside to look at the carefully packed seeds and seedlings that had come safely across the ocean. And from the neighboring towns and villages, the men came back to help once more on the farm. They worked together again tilling the soil, setting in the plants, irrigating and weeding.

"Please let them grow well," Toyoko's mother murmured each morning at the family altar.

"Don't let them die this time," Okei prayed from her hilltop each evening.

Although the winds from the mountains still held the winter's cold, the hillsides were touched now with the pale green breath of spring, and the clean damp freshness of the earth promised life for the new plantings.

Koichi wrote a long letter to his grandmother in Waka-matsu. "Herr Schnell says that everything is going to be fine now, and that when these new plants take root, we will have some fine crops and will be able to sell tea and make lacquer and wax and oil. And when the mulberry trees are growing well, we will buy silkworm seed. Then maybe the others will come from Wakamatsu. Maybe you will come too."

Koichi wrote that he was studying hard every morning, because he knew Grandmother would be pleased to hear that. "I know quite well now the language of the foreigners," he wrote, "and I am also reading Father's books of Japanese history. There is no one to fence with, and no archery or spear fighting, but Father says I will not be a warrior anyway, only a man of peace."

Koichi thought about that for a while and then added, "I suppose a person who raises tea and silkworms could be called a very peaceful man."

Koichi wondered if his letter would ever reach his grandmother. It had such a long way to go and could so easily be lost before it even reached Japan. He almost felt as though he could get his messages to Grandmother better from the top of Okei's knoll, where he sometimes went with her and Toyoko in the evening to watch the sun go to Japan. Whenever they were there, they spoke only of Wakamatsu and the people they had left behind. It was a quiet time of the day when the earth had come to rest, and they remembered Wakamatsu as it was in the days of peace.

"Of course your thoughts will reach your grandmother from here," Okei said, "just as they reach your mother and big brother in the spirit world. They are all close to you here."

"My baby sister who died too?" Toyoko asked.

"Certainly," Okei nodded.

"But she was only one when she died with the fever."

"She is a tiny spirit, but she is here too."

"It's like the Indians," Koichi said suddenly.

Toyoko looked at him questioning and puzzled, but Koichi couldn't explain it to her. He knew, however, that the Indians thought as they did. They too lived as though the dead were still close by. They gave them food and sent clothing to them in smoke. For them, too, death was just another part of life. It was all tied together.

Koichi knew that Hiram Bellweather could not understand such thoughts. He had only smiled at Okei's foolishness when he saw her put rice at the family altar, and for him the Indian burning had only been a spectacle.

It was the same with Thomas and Kate Whitlow. They really did not understand their Obon festival, even though Kate had brought fresh vegetables from their farm to help Okei decorate the altar table.

"Now, ain't it interesting that you plan a feast for your dead kinfolk," she had said, but she seemed more puzzled than anything else.

"Your customs is mighty different," she had confessed. But still, she had put her hands together and bowed in front of the altar as Okei taught her to do, because she knew it pleased Okei and Toyoko's mother.

It was not a very wet spring, but it was cool and the rains came often enough to give the new seedlings a good start. The hillsides became rolling mounds of green velvet and the bamboo trees stopped shedding their golden tears and their leaves grew green just as those on the mulberry trees.

Rintaro and the other men had gone back to their other jobs, but they would return to help when the tea was ready for picking and when the lacquer trees could be tapped. In another year the leaves of the mulberry trees would be ready for plucking and once more they could try raising their silkworms.

"At last," Father said, "I believe everything is going to be fine."

But he hadn't counted on Hiram Bellweather selling his shop, digging up his bottle of gold and moving to Sacramento.

"You're leaving Coloma?" Koichi asked, unbelieving.

Hiram nodded. "I'm buying myself a shop up Sacramento way."

"But why?" Father asked. "You have a fine shop here. Business is good. Why do you leave?"

Hiram looked flustered. He rubbed a hand across his shaggy chin and then through the mass of hair on his head. "Well, y'see," he began awkwardly, "there's a widow woman up in Sacramento. She's got a shop finer than mine. I'm going to help her run it, and I wouldn't have to cook no more meals for myself. I'd be helping out a widow woman, don't y'see?" he explained.

Father nodded. He understood.

But Koichi was worried. "Who will give us credit if you leave?" he asked.

He knew that Toyoko's mother had sold her tortoise-shell combs and ivory fan and gold hairpieces, and that Herr Schnell had even sold the dagger from Lord Matsudaira bearing his crest. Still, they needed credit from Hiram Bellweather to buy enough to eat.

"Aw, you folks ain't going to need credit for much longer," Hiram said confidently. "Why, pretty soon I might be coming down from Sacramento with my missus to buy your tea and silk for my new shop." Hiram grinned, pleased at the thought.

But Koichi couldn't feel happy no matter how he thought about it. He had lost Rintaro and now he was losing Hiram Bellweather. It wouldn't be fun coming for supplies to Coloma anymore, and Koichi would never walk to town again just to talk to Hiram.

So Hiram Bellweather left, and it was only the flowers on the hillsides that seemed to want to stay at Gold Hill. They arrived in great masses of color—bright orange poppies, purple clumps of lupine, great clusters of golden buttercups and scotch broom, and sprays of purple redbud. Toyoko and Okei would go out to gather enormous armfuls, and then Toyoko's mother would arrange them in baskets and bowls and bottles all over the house.

The sun felt good on his bones, and along with the plants in the fields, Koichi grew taller. He drank milk every day now and could eat beef and pork without hearing Grandmother's shocked voice echoing in his ear.

"We're getting to be more and more like the hairy barbarians," he said to Toyoko.

"Will our feet turn into hoofs pretty soon if we keep drinking milk and eating meat?" Toyoko asked.

"Of course not," Koichi scoffed. "Don't you know that's just a stupid tale?"

Toyoko wriggled her bare feet and went on, "I should be dreadfully sorry to lose my toes, even though the milk does taste good."

"Look at your papa's feet," Koichi said patiently. "He's a barbarian, isn't he? He's been drinking milk and eating the meat of the cow all his life."

Toyoko nodded. "But he is different."

"Why?"

"Because he is married to my Japanese mama."

"And?"

"That makes him part Japanese."

"You're stupid, Toyoko, do you know that?"

"I am not!" And Toyoko ran outside.

It was conversations such as this that made Koichi miss Rintaro and Hiram more than ever. Almost every day he went far up along the creek searching for the Maidu Indian, but even he seemed to have disappeared forever. Sometimes Koichi felt as though he didn't have a single friend in the whole world.

BIG TROUBLE AT THE CREEK

"The dry days have begun early this year," the farmers said, keeping an anxious eye on the sky. It was only May, but already the rains had stopped, and each day the sun burned hot in a bright blue sky. The soil was drying out and the hills all around had turned the color of dust.

The farmers kept the ditches cleared and the gates open so water from the creek would keep flowing into their fields. But the snows were melting too fast and by summer they would be gone.

"We must be careful," Father warned. "We must be sure there is enough water to carry us through the summer months."

They almost held their breaths, fearful that the sun and the heat would conspire again to defeat them.

And then one day at dusk, the Maidu Indian appeared at their gate. He looked thin and gaunt, and not seeing Rintaro, he spoke to Koichi.

"I look for you," Koichi said, happy to see his old friend. "Where have you been?"

"Big sickness in tribe," the Indian answered. He had been sick himself, but this was not what he had come to say.

"Big trouble up creek," he said, pointing. "White man make trouble."

"They take gold?" Koichi asked.

The Indian shook his head and made motions with his hands. "Rock upon rock," he said, gesturing. "Up creek." His voice was urgent.

"They harm your village?"

Father offered the Indian some tobacco, and Okei offered him some tea, but the Indian waved them away and only repeated what he had come to say. Then, turning, he disappeared into the woods.

"In the morning we will go up the creek to see what he means," Father said.

But in the morning it was too late. When Father and Koichi and the farmers walked up to the big creek, they found a dam of rocks and logs built securely across it, diverting the water so none of it would flow down to their land. Standing on the banks at either side of the dam were men holding rifles, and one of them was One-eye.

Koichi had almost forgotten about him. He had not bothered them since Rintaro left and Koichi had thought that he was going to leave them alone. Instead, he had only been waiting.

Now he had found the one way to destroy them all. If he took away their source of water, everything on the farm would die. He had schemed and planned with evil in his heart. He fired a shot now, shouting at them to get off his land, and they left quickly, knowing they could not reason with men holding guns.

Herr Schnell thundered into Coloma to talk to the sheriff, but the sheriff was not much help. "One-eye filed a claim to that land long ago," he said helplessly.

"But what of our rights?" Herr Schnell asked. "The creek flows through our land too."

The sheriff shrugged. "Everybody's caught by this here dry spell," he said. "Where water's concerned, it's every man for himself."

Herr Schnell went to the judge. He went to every man he knew in Coloma, but no one seemed to be able to do anything. Furthermore, no one seemed to care very much. With Hiram Bellweather gone, they seemed to have no friends left in Coloma. Everyone seemed to have turned against them.

"Why?" Father asked Thomas Whitlow. "We have worked hard. We have made no trouble for anyone."

But Thomas had no answer either. "Everybody needs water bad now, and I suppose the white men feel they deserve first chance at it."

"Ah," Father said, "so that is it. In that case, we have lost."

One-eye had won after all. He had said they'd be sorry they ever came to Gold Hill, and now maybe he would be right.

Koichi wanted to challenge him with their swords. "I know we could win," he told Father.

But Father shook his head. "That is not the answer, Koichi," he said.

There seemed to be no answer at all. Toyoko's mother sold her finest embroidered silk coat and one day Father's second sword was gone.

Koichi knew now that there was something he could do, that he *had* to do for the colony. He took Grandfather's samurai sword down from the closet shelf and drew it from its lacquered sheath. The gold inlay on the sword guard had grown a little dull, but the blade was still razor sharp as it gleamed in the sunlight. Koichi remembered how Grandmother had told him the finest swordmaker in all of Wakamatsu had forged the sword especially for Grandfather. He held the sword high and swung it down on his imaginary enemy.

"*Yah!*" he struck One-eye's arm.

"*Yoi!*" he whacked at his ear.

"*Yai! Kora!*" He showed no mercy. He would not allow One-eye to die honorably with his own hand. He thrust his sword straight into his evil scheming heart. "There!"

Koichi put the sword back into its sheath, touched it lightly with his fingers and then put it on Father's bed. It was not a sack of gold, but it was all he had to give. Father would know what to do with it.

When Father saw him later, he said simply, "Thank you, Koichi. I know how much the sword meant to you."

And the next time the adults met to speak of their plans for the future, Koichi was invited to sit with them.

"You have contributed as a man," Herr Schnell said, "and now you shall have the voice of a man."

Koichi knew then that One-eye had not succeeded in destroying him after all. Now, he could take his place next to Father and the other men, and would face any new disappointments without flinching. Herr Schnell had said he was a man. His sword was gone, but he would not mourn its loss, for he had lost it not in defeat, but in honor.

One day Herr Schnell gathered them all together, as he had done on the day he read the deed to them. This time, however, his eyes were older and sadder and the look of hope was gone.

"Good friends," he said, not knowing how to begin. "Our money is almost gone . . . our plants do not grow, for it is impossible to raise enough water now from the streams below, and our creek has been dammed. The rains do not come," he went on, "and the townspeople have turned against us. All I can do now is return to Japan and seek more money from Lord Matsudaira. Then I shall return with more plants, and we will begin again."

He paused for a long time, looking down at his feet. "I have decided to take my wife and child and leave immediately. But we will return. Please be patient. Wait for us."

No one spoke. What was there to say? Herr Schnell looked like a general who had lost a war.

"We will wait for your return," Father said at last. "Those who can will find jobs elsewhere, but Koichi and I will wait for you here."

Koichi spoke later to Okei. "Are you going back with them?" he asked.

Okei was not sure. "Herr Schnell said I could go if I wish."

"Oh, come with us," Toyoko begged. "Who will take care of me?"

"But who will take care of Koichi-san and his father if I go?" Okei asked.

Who would indeed? Koichi felt a chill at the mere thought of being without Okei.

All that day Okei struggled, trying to decide the right thing. More than anything in the world, she longed to go home, but she knew that she was needed at Gold Hill even more than she was at home.

The next morning, Koichi looked to see if Okei had packed her belongings, but she had not. And when he went into the kitchen she was cooking breakfast as she always did.

"You're staying then?" he asked eagerly.

Okei nodded. "How would you or your father ever get this stove lighted if I left?" she asked, with a smile. "And who would make the porridge you like so well?"

Koichi grinned. He wished he could do something wonderful for Okei. Finally, he said, "I'll go catch you the biggest salmon you ever saw in your whole life. You wait and see."

And so Herr Schnell and Toyoko and her mother left without Okei, and Father drove them in the wagon to Folsom to catch the Sacramento Valley Railroad into town.

"Oh, Okei, I wish you were coming with us," Toyoko wept.

Okei gathered her in her arms and whispered, "My heart is going with you, Toyo-chan, and one day, the rest of me will follow. You wait for me."

"But we'll be back before then, won't we?"

"Perhaps," Okei said softly, "only perhaps."

"Take care of yourselves," Toyoko's mother said almost in a whisper. Her hair was no longer combed into the elegant style she had worn when she arrived, and now she might even be mistaken in Japan for a farmer's wife or a servant. She said nothing of seeing them again.

"Safe journey," Koichi called to them. It seemed strange that he felt sorry to see Toyoko leaving.

"I will write," Herr Schnell promised as he climbed into the wagon. "I promise to write."

Father clucked at the horses and soon the wagon rattled out of the yard and onto the road. What a long journey lay ahead of them, Koichi thought. It would be a long, long time before they set foot again on Japanese soil.

"Good-bye . . . *sayonara*. . . ." Toyoko's thin voice came back to them from the road.

And then the wagon disappeared around the bend. They were gone, and the world suddenly seemed a very empty place.

END OF A DREAM

Father was now the leader of the Wakamatsu Colony, or what was left of it. There were only two farmers who remained, and they did not have much to do. They wanted to draw water up from the streams below, but there was no money to buy the lumber and equipment they would need to build pumps and flumes to carry the water up to their land.

Instead of the vast acres of farmland, they now tended their small vegetable patch, watering it one bucketful at a time with water from the well. They grew cucumbers and potatoes and carrots and turnips. And after they had carefully plucked every weed that appeared among the vegetables, they went down to the streams to catch fish for their supper.

Koichi usually went with them. But sometimes he went with Okei to the Whitlow ranch. Kate was teaching Okei how to make preserves and jelly and how to pickle cucumbers and bake bread. She never failed to give Koichi a generous sample of whatever they made, and sent them home with extra jars of pickles and preserves.

They all tried to keep busy, but mostly, it was a time of waiting. They counted the days until Herr Schnell would reach Japan. Then they counted the days until he would reach Wakamatsu.

"Perhaps this very day he is seeing Lord Matsudaira," Father said one day, and then they began to wait for his letter. All through the searing hot dry summer months they waited. And again the hills and fields turned brown, looking like bread baked in the hot ovens of summer.

Then, one day, Rintaro came back from a job he had found in Placerville.

"Rintaro!" Koichi shouted. "You've come back."

Rintaro grinned sheepishly. "Only for a visit," he said. "I came, in fact, to tell your father of a fine opportunity I have."

"You've found a new job?" Father asked.

"I have a chance to buy my way into a business in Placerville," he explained. "It is just a small shop—a general store—but it is a beginning. It is a chance to make good." He stopped.

"Then you won't ever come back to the farm?" Koichi asked.

"I'll come back for visits, of course," Rintaro said, but he promised no more. Furthermore, he wasn't finished with what he had come to say.

"I . . . that is, I . . . uh, have also met a fine woman who says . . . well, it could be that . . . maybe I have found myself a wife. She is a good woman. I do not drink so much anymore."

Rintaro was embarrassed to speak of such good fortune which had come only to him. He wiped the sweat from his face with the back of his hand and looked down at his feet.

Father put a hand on his shoulder. "Go make a good life for yourself in Placerville, Rintaro," he said. "I am happy for you. I wish you well."

This time when Rintaro packed, he took everything, and Koichi knew he would not come back even when Herr Schnell returned.

"He's gone for good," he said glumly to Okei.

"Perhaps," she said.

And then she turned to Koichi and said something so wise, it sounded like something his grandmother would have said.

"You know, Koichi-san," she said, "we all have a special place in life, and when we find it, we must accept it. My place and your place is here in Gold Hill. But Rintaro's is now in Placerville. It is fate. Don't you see? That is how it is, and you must let him go and be happy for him."

Koichi dug his toe into the dirt and made ever-widening circles with his foot. "I'll let him go," he said grudgingly, "but I won't be happy about it."

Okei continued hanging out her wash, and when she had finished, she said simply, "You know, your father was very proud of you when you gave up your sword."

Then, she moved quickly into the house and left Koichi pondering in the sun, still making lonely circles in the dirt. He did not go inside until the sun had dropped low in the sky.

After Rintaro, the others left as well, even the last two farmers, who found work on other farms. They promised to return when Herr Schnell came back, but Koichi saw that they took all their belongings with them. At last only Father and Koichi and Okei were left, like the last autumn leaves clinging stubbornly to a barren tree. And still there was no letter from Herr Schnell.

Their farm looked now like the dried carcasses left on the gold rush trails, and more and more, the weeds took over where the plantings had died.

At last, one day, Thomas Whitlow came to talk with Father. He still wore his work clothes and his boots were covered with the dust of the fields. Okei made him a cup of coffee and they all sat at the kitchen table.

"He's not coming back, you know," Thomas said quietly.
"Who?" Father asked.
"Herr Schnell."

"But he promised. He gave his word. He asked us to wait."

Thomas pulled out a big blue handkerchief from his pocket and wiped his face with it. "Maybe he meant to come back—he probably did—but if he was coming, he'd of written a letter at least by now."

Father nodded. "That is true."

Father did not want to believe it, but deep in his heart he knew that Thomas Whitlow was right.

"Perhaps it is time now to face the truth," Father said gravely.

Thomas nodded. "I was hoping you would," he said. He looked earnestly at Father's face and added, "It'll soon be winter and then there won't be much work. But right now, I hear tell there's a big wheat farm out Sacramento way that's looking for hands. If you was to go now, you could get work and make some money. Maybe there'd be work for the boy too."

"And what of our farm?" Father asked. "What of Okei?"

"Why, we'd take Okei and keep her as long as she wants," Thomas answered quickly. "Kate loves her like a daughter. I only wish we could take the both of you in too."

"And our farm?" Koichi reminded him. *cop.3*

"I'll keep an eye on it for you. I'll let you know first thing if ever a letter does come from Herr Schnell. What do you say, Mr. Matsuzaka?" Thomas asked urgently. "You and the boy got to eat. You got to have a warm place come winter. You got to make a living somehow."

Father looked tired and sad and lonely. His face was creased with lines from worry and long days in the sun. He sat looking out the window for a long time, and then he asked Thomas Whitlow to give him one day to think about it. "Tomorrow I will give you an answer," he said.

That night Father spoke to Koichi. "It is a difficult thing to accept defeat," he said slowly, "but sometimes a good samurai must accept it with grace. We did our best. We tried hard, but perhaps this farm was simply not meant to be."

Koichi nodded. Maybe Okei had been wrong. Maybe Gold Hill was not meant to be their special place in life, after all.

"I guess our place in life is somewhere else," he said, not knowing what to say.

Father brightened. "You are right, Koichi," he said. "We will move on and we will become good farmers elsewhere. We will find our special place somewhere. You'll see." And straightening his shoulders as he might before riding off to battle, Father began to think about leaving Gold Hill.

Now it was Koichi and Father and Okei who packed their belongings. They cleaned out the house and left it just as they had found it that sunny day long ago.

Thomas Whitlow came to take them to Sacramento in his wagon, and Kate Whitlow came to get Okei. They stood beside the cedar sapling they had planted the day the deed had been signed. It was the only thing that had withstood the heat and had not perished as everything else. It was all that remained of the Wakamatsu Colony's efforts.

Father bowed to Okei as he would have to another samurai. "You are a fine woman, Okei," he said. "I thank you for your loyalty and for your sacrifice, and especially for your loving heart."

Okei returned his bow. "I only did what I knew was right," she murmured.

Then, taking Koichi's hand, she said softly, "You will always be a brave samurai, Koichi-san, no matter where you go or what you do. I know that. And someday, we will all go home to Wakamatsu. I know that too." She smiled briefly and then added, "Don't forget me."

Koichi shook his head. "I will never forget you, Okei," he said.

"Be a good lad now," Kate Whitlow said, kissing him on the cheek. "And come back here whenever you've a mind to."

Father took one last look inside the mailbox. It was still empty.

The good-byes were over. They climbed into the wagon and Thomas Whitlow called to the horses to get them on their way. They rattled slowly over the dusty road, leaving once more on the very wagon they had ridden the day they had arrived.

"Good-bye, Mrs. Whitlow . . . *sayonara*, Okei. . . ." Koichi waved as long as he could, watching first the Graner house and then Gold Hill disappear behind him.

A hawk wheeled high in the sky above them, screeching noisily at something on the ground.

"Well, I reckon it's going to be another scorcher," Thomas Whitlow said, squinting up at the sun.

But Father didn't seem to hear him. "It was a noble dream while it lasted," he said quietly. And he looked straight ahead, just as he had on the day they started out from Wakamatsu so long ago. He didn't look back then, and he didn't look back now.

Koichi sat tall in the seat beside Father, and he too looked straight ahead down the road. It was time now to think about what lay ahead. It was time now to think about their new life, for the Wakamatsu Colony was no more, and soon, it would only be the dim memory of a golden dream.

Author's Note

During the years following World War I, when many Japanese farmers were settling in the area of Coloma, California, one of them happened to stumble upon an old marble tombstone at the top of a grassy knoll. The stone was almost buried under a heavy growth of weeds and wild roses, but when it was uncovered, it revealed the following brief inscription:

IN MEMORY OF OKEI
DIED 1871, AGED 19 YEARS
A JAPANESE GIRL

No one knew who she was or why she was buried there so far from her homeland. A Japanese newspaperman, determined to learn more of this young girl, began to inquire among the people who lived nearby. Fortunately, he met the family who not only knew Okei, but knew about the Wakamatsu Colony as well. And thus was uncovered a fascinating story which began in Japan in 1869.

About the time when the gold rush was over in California, a period of chaos of an entirely different kind was taking place in Japan. After almost two hundred years of isolation and relative peace under the rule of the Shogunate, the feudal system was beginning to collapse. The clans of the south, opposed to the westerners whom the Shogun was allowing into the country, rallied around the cry, "Oust the barbarians and restore the Emperor."

The Emperor, who, until now, was only a figurehead in the Kyoto Palace, was restored, and the Shogun relinquished all his powers to him. The northern clans who had supported the Shogun were mercilessly defeated by the clans of the south. One of the last of the northern clans to surrender was the Aizu Clan of Wakamatsu, led by Lord Katamori Matsudaira. Although they fought valiantly, Wakamatsu castle fell in November, 1868, and the city was reduced to rubble.

Among Lord Matsudaira's trusted advisors was a Prussian, J. Henry Schnell, an importer who had supplied arms to the north. Believing, perhaps, that California offered a bright future as it turned from its preoccupation with gold to the production of agriculture, he suggested to Lord Matsudaira that he be permitted to take a group of colonists from Wakamatsu to Gold Hill, California, to establish a tea and silk farm. He hoped, someday, that Lord Matsudaira himself might be able to flee there for sanctuary.

And so a small band of colonists made its way to California, taking along trees and saplings and seeds of their native land to establish their ill-fated farm. Coming as they did from the formal feudal society of Japan and being plunged into the boisterous, crude life of post–gold rush California, the fact that they persevered as long as they did seems a great tribute to their courage and patience.

This much is fact. The rest of my story is as I have imagined life might have been for them, as there are virtually no records of how the colonists existed. My characters, except for those named above, are fictitious.

It is also fact that these people were the first of many other pioneer immigrants who, in later years, came to the United States from Japan and contributed much to the tremendous agricultural development of California. The site of the Wakamatsu Tea and Silk Farm was named a California Historical Landmark in 1969, and on a hill near the monument, Okei's small tombstone still stands.

I am greatly indebted to Mrs. E. W. Sayre, of Sacramento, who for many years painstakingly researched the story of the Wakamatsu Colony. She took me to the site of the Wakamatsu Colony farm and most generously shared with me all of her valuable research material.

I am also grateful to Mr. Ferol Egan for suggesting that this story be written and for checking my manuscript regarding certain aspects of California history.

—Y.U.

Glossary

AIZU	*eye-zoo*	Name of clan in Waka-matsu.
BANDAI-AZUMA	*bahn-dye ah-zoo-mah*	Mountains surrounding Wakamatsu.
CHAN	*chahn*	Term of endearment used for children, as in Ko-chan.
EDO	*eh-doh*	Name of Tokyo until 1868.
FUROSHIKI	*foo-roh-shee-kee*	Square cloth used to wrap and carry small objects.
HAIKU	*high-koo*	Seventeen-syllable Japanese poem.
ISE	*ee-seh*	Name of town where one of Japan's major shrines is located.
KIMONO	*kee-moh-noh*	Japanese dress, male or female.
KIRI	*kee-ree*	Wood of paulownia tree.
KOICHI	*koh-ee-chee*	Son of Matsuzaka, Gentai.
KORA	*koh-rah*	Exclamation, such as "hey."
KYOTO	*kyo-toh*	Former palace city of the Emperor.
MAH, MAH	*mah, mah*	Expression, such as "my, my."
MATSUDAIRA, KATAMORI	*mah-tsoo-dye-rah, kah-tah-moh-ree*	Lord of Wakamatsu at the time of this story.
MATSUZAKA, GENTAI	*mah-tsoo-zah-kah, gen-tye*	Koichi's father. The Japanese custom is to give the surname first. The "g" is hard, as in "gas."

OBON	*oh-bon*	Midsummer festival of returning spirits.
ODEN	*oh-den*	Broth containing many vegetables.
OI	*oy*	Exclamation, such as "hey."
OKEI	*oh-kay-ee*	Servant to the Schnell family.
RINTARO	*rin-tah-roh*	Name of carpenter. In feudal days, people such as farmers and craftsmen had no surnames.
SAH, SAH	*sah, sah*	Expression, such as "come, come," or "come, now."
SAKE	*sah-keh*	Japanese rice wine.
SAMURAI	*sah-moo-rye*	Warrior and highest-ranking class of feudal period. The samurai often helped govern the lord's fief.
SAN	*sahn*	Added to a person's name, it is a polite form of address, as in Koichi-san.
SAYONARA	*sah-yoh-nah-rah*	"Good-bye."
SHOGUN	*show-goon*	Military ruler of Japan during the feudal period.
TASUKETE	*tah-soo-keh-teh*	"Help me."
TATAMI	*tah-tah-mee*	Thick rush mat laid over the floor.
TOKYO	*to-kyoh*	Capital of Japan.
TOYOKO	*toh-yoh-koh*	Daughter of J. Henry Schnell.
WAKAMATSU	*wah-kah-mah-tsoo*	Town in northern Japan, now called Aizu-wakamatsu.
YAH, YAI, YOI	*yah, yah-ee, yoh-ee*	Exclamations.

YOISHO	*yoi-shoh*	Exclamation often used when doing heavy work.
YOKOHAMA	*yoh-koh-hah-mah*	Major port city of Japan.

Japanese words are pronounced without accenting any syllables and all letters are sounded. Throughout the book, only those Japanese words not included in *Webster's Seventh New Collegiate Dictionary* have been italicized.